SOLDIER

SHIPWRECK ON THE HIGH SEAS

DOGS

READ ALL THE

SOLDIER DOGS

BOOKS!

SOLDIER

SHIPWRECK ON THE HIGH SEAS

DOGS

MARCUS SUTTER

ILLUSTRATIONS BY ANDIE TONG

HARPER FESTIVAL

An Imprint of HarperCollinsPublishers

Library of Congress Cataloging-in-Publication Data

Names: Sutter, Marcus, author. | Tong, Andie, illustrator.
Title: Shipwreck on the high seas / Marcus Sutter ; illustrations by Andie Tong.
Description: First edition. | New York, NY : HarperFestival, an imprint of
HarperCollins Publishers, [2020] | Series: Soldier dogs ; #7 | Audience: Ages 8-12. |
Audience: Grades 4-6. | Summary: Several months after Pearl Harbor, cabin boy Julio
and his loyal Boxer Jack fight to survive after their merchant marine ship is torpedoed
by German U-boats. Includes historical facts and a timeline of World War II.
Identifiers: LCCN 2020000862 | ISBN 978-0-06-295799-3 (pbk.)
Subjects: CYAC: Survival—Fiction. | Boxer (Dog breed)—Fiction. | Dogs—Fiction. |
Orphans—Fiction. | Merchant marine—Fiction. | World War, 1939-1945—Fiction. |
Cuban Americans—Fiction.
Classification: LCC PZ7.1.S8837 Sh 2020 | DDC [Fic]—dc23
LC record available at https://lccn.loc.gov/2020000862

Typography by Rick Farley
20 21 22 23 24   PC/LSCH   10 9 8 7 6 5 4 3 2 1
❖
First Edition

For the brave crew, both two-footed and four-footed, of the US Merchant Marine. You are truly heroes.

PROLOGUE

THURSDAY, MAY 22, 1943
4:52 A.M. LOCAL TIME

Julio's heart hammered in his chest.

The bridge and the wheelhouse, where Captain Bayne stood every day guiding the *Susquehanna* and her crew, were completely gone. Smoke billowed from belowdecks. Cannons thundered in the distance.

Julio froze with panic. He knew the merchant marine ship had been hit at least twice by German U-boat torpedoes. Any second, they could be hit by another one—the one that could sink the ship.

The ship's whistle sounded two long blasts

followed by a short one. The signal for distress.

"Captain Bayne must still be alive, Jack," Julio said to his dog. "Everything will be okay."

No answering bark.

Julio looked behind him. No Jack.

He looked on either side. No Jack.

"Jack!" Julio shouted above the noise. "Jack!"

Julio's heart froze with fear. Where was his dog?

Someone bumped into him. Spud Campbell, the third cook, stumbled past Julio, his eyes wide and uncomprehending.

Julio grabbed Spud's arm. "Have you seen Jack?"

Spud looked at him like he was a total stranger. Like they hadn't played endless games of dice together, like Spud hadn't been one of Jack's favorite people. He pulled his arm from Julio's grasp. "They're gone," he said, shaking his head. "Every one of them's gone." And then, before Julio could ask who "them" was, Spud hurried away.

An explosion in the engine room shook the ship hard.

Julio was thrown to the deck.

"No!" Julio cried. He staggered to his feet. His legs carried him to the back of the crazily tilting ship as if taking on a mind of their own. Maybe Jack was waiting for him at their designated lifeboat. Jack was smart. He'd know to do that if they got separated, wouldn't he?

Julio stared in disbelief. No Jack. No lifeboat. Just a tangle of useless cables and ropes. And the lifeboats on the other side of the ship were gone or useless too.

The *Susquehanna* lurched and tilted to one side like a wounded animal.

Julio's blood turned to ice. He had to find Jack and get off the boat. It was sinking fast!

Suddenly, Julio heard a familiar bark.

"Jack!" the boy cried. "Where are you?"

Smoke billowed up through the large forward hatch cover.

He heard a splash.

"Jack!"

He ran to the starboard side. A hole big enough to drive a supply truck through had been blown into the side, exactly where the engine room was. Water poured into the ship.

In the sea below, a lifeboat full of crew rowed frantically away from the *Susquehanna*.

"Hey!" Julio called down, waving his arms. "Hey! Don't leave us!"

The face of Sarge, the ship's bosun, looked up at him. Sarge was the boss of the ordinary and able seamen. He'd tell them to wait for him.

"There's another lifeboat on the port side," Sarge called. "Get it down and get away from the ship as quick as you can!"

"But it was—"

"We'll look for you, Julio, but we've got to get away from the ship. She's sinking fast!"

Julio leaned as far as he dared over the side of the boat and watched in horror as his only hope rowed away.

CHAPTER 1

Julio and Jack stretched out on the open deck above the ship's bridge, the sun-warmed steel pressing into their bellies.

Julio held binoculars to his eyes, scanning the open sea for any signs of danger. He'd been a cabin boy on the merchant marine Liberty ship the *Susquehanna* for over a year. Julio knew these ships faced many dangers every day. From fierce storms to enemy aircraft and underwater mines, danger was never far. But nothing was as deadly as the German U-boats, silently prowling

underneath the waters. Hundreds of merchant marine ships had been torpedoed and sunk by Nazi submarines during the war.

"Not on my watch," Julio said to Jack.

Beside him, his dog, Jack, yawned and scratched lazily behind his ear with his back leg. He was tired from rat-hunting duty the night before.

Through the binoculars, Julio saw the other ships in the convoy about six hundred yards to the side and behind the *Susquehanna*. Farther out, about a thousand yards, a warship and two radar ships protected the important cargo aboard the merchant marines ships.

Being part of a convoy always made Julio feel a little safer on the open ocean. But this time Julio not only felt safer, he felt proud: the commodore, captain of the entire convoy, was stationed on the *Susquehanna* for this very important mission.

Julio knew the two radar ships were sweeping the area for any signs of danger from the skies or beneath the sea.

"But radar ships can never replace the keen eyes, constant vigilance, and sharp instincts of a merchant marine seaman," Captain Bayne always said.

Julio rubbed the sun-warmed side of Jack.

"Between my eyes and your ears, we're the best watch team on the boat," Julio said to Jack. "Probably in the whole convoy."

Jack sneezed in agreement and licked his boy's hand.

Julio had hurried through his morning duties—helping the galley staff serve the crew breakfast and cleaning up after, taking coffee-filled thermoses to the men on their four-hour watch duties, sweeping out the crew's quarters, and wiping down the bridge—so he could spend extra time watching for trouble before his evening duties began.

In Julio's mind, a familiar movie played: He spots the periscope of a Nazi U-boat before any-one else on the ship does and saves the entire convoy. Captain Bayne puts his arm around Julio and says, "Son, you're a true American hero." Not just an orphaned Cuban American kid nobody wanted.

Julio took the compass from his pocket and

checked the direction.

The compass had belonged to his father, some-one he had very little memory of. His father had been a sailor, and rarely home. Julio did remember the spicy smell of bay rum aftershave and strong, dark brown hands throwing him high into the air. Even those memories were fading, though.

Julio studied the compass's arrow. Due south and just a hair east. Exactly the direction they'd been going ever since they left the port in Savan-nah, Georgia, two weeks before.

"Hey, boy," a gruff voice called from below. "What are you doing with those binoculars?"

Julio groaned. Jack growled. They both knew that voice all too well. It was Jeramiah O'Brien, the new ship carpenter who had joined the crew in Savannah. He was given the nickname Chips, just like every ship's carpenter. But Julio had liked the previous Chips a lot better.

"Just watching for trouble, sir," Julio replied. Most of the lower-ranking crew didn't insist Julio call them sir, but this guy did. Worst of all, the man had taken an immediate dislike to Jack. Julio couldn't understand it. Everyone on ship loved

Jack. Captain Bayne had even given him the merchant marine rank of able seaman, because Jack was always ready to do what needed to be done.

"Not your job, boy," Chips said, glaring up at him. "You best get down here and quit your lollygagging and daydreaming. There's rust on the port side to be scraped."

Julio watched the Irishman limp away. He did one last visual sweep with his binoculars, then climbed down to the main deck. Jack followed down the steep stairs, nimble as a cat.

Julio sighed. "Quit your lollygagging and daydreaming," he said to Jack in a perfect imitation of Chips's thick Irish accent.

It was the rare quiet time on the ship. Most everyone above decks had done their jobs. In the *Susquehanna*'s engine room, though, the work was never done. Those not on their four-hour assigned watch relaxed, at least for a little while. Second Mate Walt Semenov sat in the shade of the bridge, reading from his endless supply of paperback westerns. First Mate Harvie played cards with Third Mate Rick "Hollywood" Hansome.

Julio trotted toward the port side of the ship, Jack on his heels.

"Hey, Julio," Able Seaman Jamaica called. He rattled the dice in his hand. "Come play five thousand with us." Sarge sat cross-legged on the floor. That was one of the things Julio loved about the merchant marine: during downtime, everyone was of equal rank. As the ship's bosun, Sarge was the boss of all the men working on the main deck, including Jamaica. But when they weren't working, the two could always be found together, playing cards or dice.

Julio groaned. "Can't. *Chips* says I have work to do." Why did Chips pick on him anyway?

"Tough luck, man," Jamaica said. "Don't know what that guy's beef is."

"How about you, Jack?" Sarge patted the space next to him.

Jack looked up at Julio with his big brown eyes, his eyebrows quirked in a question.

"Go on, boy," Julio said, giving him a pat on the shoulder. "One of us should have fun."

Jack licked his boy's hand. He trotted over to Sarge and plopped down by his side. The men grinned and rubbed Jack's ears for good luck.

Julio found a scraper in a storage box. He scanned the port side of the ship, looking for rust.

"Over there, by the lifeboats."

Julio jumped. He hadn't heard Chips come up behind him.

"I lowered one of the boats," Chips said, pointing to the wooden lifeboat resting against the side of the ship. "Get in and get all that rust where the boat has been. After you've finished, come get me. I'll lower the other one."

"Yes, sir," Julio said.

"And keep your mind to it," Chips said.

Julio sighed. He didn't mind scraping rust when it was needed. He even kind of liked it: it gave him time to think, to "daydream," as Chips called it.

He hadn't known to even daydream about such a thing when he lived in the orphanage outside of Savannah, Georgia. He'd been taken there when he was five, after his parents were killed in a car crash. He had no other relatives in America, but his parents had made sure their one and only child was born in the US of A.

The first few years in the orphanage, Julio had daydreamed someone would come and make him part of their family. They wouldn't care that he had dark skin and a foreign-sounding name. They would see that he was special, that he and only he was the one they needed to complete their family.

People came and went, looking for a child to take home. Time after time, Julio was not chosen. Time after time, his heart was broken.

Over the years, the dream of a family faded, just like the memories of his parents. Still, he always carried his father's compass in his pocket. When they visited the public library, Julio studied the same books on sailing. In those books, he learned how to use the compass, how to tie knots every sailor should know, how to use a signal mirror. In those books, he held on to some slim thread of his family.

Finally, tired of waiting for someone to adopt him, Julio decided to take matters into his own hands. During an outing to the library, he slipped away, leaving the orphanage and all the taunting and loneliness behind. His father's compass pointed the way east, the way to Savannah, to what he thought would be an easier life. "Boy, was I ever wrong," Julio whispered to himself.

Julio felt a heavy thump. His heart leaped into his throat as the lifeboat rocked and swayed. He grabbed for a rope as the angry face of Chips flashed in his mind. He was going to fall overboard!

CHAPTER 2

Julio cried out in alarm. Jack smelled Julio's fear and nudged Julio's hand with his wet nose. He smelled relief washing over the boy like a gentle wave.

Jack had followed Julio's scent to the lifeboat and jumped inside after he'd gotten bored watching the men place dice. They were nice enough, especially when they had treats in their pockets. But he never liked being away from Julio for long.

Julio steadied the boat, then kneeled down beside Jack. He stroked his side and whispered in Jack's ears. Jack didn't understand all the boy's words, but he didn't need to. He could feel from Julio's hands and the smell on his skin everything he needed to know. His boy was a little angry and sad. Jack lifted his head and licked the boy's face to make sure salt water wasn't leaking from Julio's eyes.

This was Jack's most important job: taking care of his boy. It had been so ever since the two found each other down by the wharves in Savannah. Jack had lived there on his own for as long as he could remember. He had a distant memory of his mother's milky scent, brothers and sisters pushing him, the runt of the litter, away from his mother's milk. Jack was always hungry.

But Jack was a survivor. And like all boxers, Jack was brave and smart. He learned the best places to search the garbage for food. He also learned that other dogs were his competition for food, so Jack became a good fighter. That also meant he became a loner. At night, he curled up inside one of the many storage sheds lining the docks. Alone.

Until one stormy night. As thunder shook the

ground and lightning slashed the sky, Jack cowered in the far corner of a shed, shivering. He would never understand that deafening boom of the thunder, the sound of the sky being split in two. He wasn't afraid of much, but his brave heart pounded a mile a minute during these storms.

A movement at the door. Something wet and frightened slipped in. Jack spread his nostrils wide, searching for the intruder's scent. A human. A boy. A boy every bit as scared as he was.

Thunder crashed, rattling the shed's metal roof. Jack whimpered. Without a word, the boy crossed over to him, held his hand out for a sniff. Jack could smell kindness and yearning on him. Jack knew this boy was as much a stray as he was.

The boy sat down next to Jack. He stroked Jack's broad, square head and fine, pointed ears, over and over. The boy whispered to him, hummed to him. They both stopped shivering.

The next morning when Jack awoke, he found himself tangled in the boy's arms. He licked his dirty face. The boy opened his eyes. Brown eyes stared into even browner eyes. The boy smiled. "Hi," he said.

Jack wagged his nub of a tail. *Hey, kiddo.*

From then on, the two were never apart. They ate together, played together, fought together, they were a family. No longer strays, as long as they had each other.

Jack watched Julio scrape the rust off the ship. As much as he loved being with his boy, watching him scrape rust was not the most exciting game.

Jack barked. He lowered his chest down to the bottom of the boat, his back end sticking high in the air. He woofed again, hopefully.

"Sorry, Jack," Julio said. "If Chips catches me playing with you, it's no telling what he'll do."

Jack sighed. He sniffed under the lifeboat's benches and under the canvas sail for rats. No rats today. Instead, he pulled out a canvas pouch and tossed it in the air.

Julio grabbed the pouch. But instead of throwing it back for a game of catch, Julio frowned. "This is the signal mirror, Jack, not a toy," he scolded.

Jack snorted. Not only was his boy boring, he was no fun! With barely a backward glance, Jack leaped from the lifeboat. Time for his other jobs. His second most important job was rat patrol. The cat in the galley was fat and useless, but Jack had become an excellent rat hunter on the docks.

"See you, Jack!" the boy called.

Jack trotted down to the galley where the ship's cook, Stewie, and his assistant, Spud Campbell, peeled potatoes for the crew's dinner.

"Hey there, Jack," Stewie said with a smile. "Am I glad to see you! Looks like a rat got into the bags of corn again."

Jack glared at the cat, lounging on top of a crate of powered eggs. *You're about as useful as a flea.* The cat flicked the end of her tail and yawned.

Jack smelled a rat hiding behind a small barrel of cooking oil. He crouched and waited. Sure enough, the rat scurried out from its hiding place. Jack lunged, his jaws wide. The rat shot into the air, trying to escape onto a wooden chopping block. But boxers are excellent jumpers. Jack sprang off his back legs like a kangaroo and grabbed the rat.

"Great job, Jack!" Stewie gave him a plate of lunch leftovers.

After Jack finished lunch, he took the stairs

down to the engine room. Now came his third most important job: checking on his crew.

Jack didn't really like the engine room. It was loud with its huge, whirling cranks, gleaming piston rods sliding and thumping in and out of cylinders. The roaring fires in the furnaces made the room too hot. Still, the crew in the engine room were always happy to see him.

The oiler, Rags, wiped the sweat from his face and grinned at the sight of the dog. "Hiya, big guy!" He dug one greasy hand into his pocket, then held two fists out to Jack. "Which one?"

With his powerful sense of smell, this game was far too easy for Jack.

Jack sniffed one fist and then the other. He tilted his head to one side, as if considering the matter. Which he wasn't. He knew.

The men held their breath as Jack considered. Then he slapped Rag's left fist with his paw and barked.

"Hurray!" the men all cheered. Jack wagged his tail and ate the piece of bread. It didn't take much to make the engine room crew happy.

Jack climbed the stairs up away from the noise

and heat to the midship house where the crew lived. He trotted up the steep wooden stairs to the main deck of the ship. The air was deliciously cool and full of salty scents. Heaven!

Jack found Chief Engineer Harrison perched atop one of the many supply trucks chained to the deck of the ship. The engineer scanned the endless sea with his binoculars.

Jack let out a soft *woof.*

Harrison lowered his binoculars and grinned down at Jack.

"Hey, Jack! I'll be right down." The man scrambled down the side of the truck with ease. Jack wagged his tail and grinned.

The chief engineer patted Jack's head. "Boy am I glad you're here. This three p.m. to seven p.m. watch shift seems to go on forever." He scratched Jack in that perfect spot behind his ear. Jack leaned against the man's leg and sighed with pleasure.

"Of course, boring is better than nerve-racking," the chief engineer said. "I wouldn't tell this to anybody else, Jack, but the shifts at dawn and dusk when the sky and the ocean are that same gray color give me the jitters. Everything looks like the plume of a torpedo or the top of a U-boat."

Chief Engineer Harrison reached into the pocket of his pants. Jack wagged his tail hopefully. But instead of a tasty treat, the man pulled something small and flat from his pocket.

The man touched the something with his finger tenderly. "It's my boy's birthday tomorrow, Jack. He'll be six years old. I wonder what kind of cake my Jenny will make for him?"

Jack rested his head on the man's knee. He felt Harrison's sadness. He nudged his hand with his wet nose. Harrison smiled just a bit. He stroked the white blaze between Jack's ears and told him all about *his* boy, a boy named Todd.

"You two would be best pals, Jack, I just know you would." At the sound of his name, Jack grinned up at the man.

"When this war is over and I'm home for good, I think I'm going to get us a dog. Every boy needs a dog, right, Jack?"

Somewhere far off—too far for the man's ears—Jack heard the sound of a whale blowing water as it surfaced. And somewhere, even farther still, Jack smelled a storm on the wind. A big one.

CHAPTER 3

The next morning, word spread like wild-fire aboard the ship: the convoy commodore would address the entire crew at 1300 hours. Few of the crew had seen much of the commodore since they'd left port in Savannah ten days before. He spent many hours on the *Susquehanna*'s main bridge putting all the convoy ships through endless emergency drills. One signal flag meant a change in speed, another meant an immediate change of course. Everyone had to be ready for any possible emergency, whether by sea, or by air, or by Mother Nature.

Julio dug through the steamer trunk at the foot of his bed. "I know it's here somewhere," he muttered. Finally, he saw it, glowing white in the bottom of the trunk: a sailor cap Captain Bayne had given him after their first trip across the North Atlantic to Portugal. It had been a particularly rough crossing with waves as big as mountains. Julio hadn't gotten seasick once, unlike many of the crew, including Jack. "You've earned it, son," Captain Bayne had said, presenting him with the cap. Julio hadn't known which he was prouder of: the cap or being called "son."

Julio set the cap on his head just so and smoothed down his white shirt. He'd grown a bit since he'd last worn it. The cuffs came well above his brown wrists now. Julio rolled up the sleeves. Then he checked the pockets of his pants for the two things he was never without: his father's compass and the three-blade pocket knife every crew member, from cabin boy to captain, carried.

"Now your turn, Jack." He brushed the boxer's brown coat until it shined. He scrubbed the white patch on his chest and the white socks on the dog's legs with a wet rag.

Julio sat back on his heels and studied Jack through narrowed eyes. He sighed. "That'll have to do, I guess." He took the red, white, and blue handkerchief he kept for special occasions and tied it around the dog's neck.

"Let's go, Jack!"

The entire crew stood at attention in the hot sun on the midship deck. The crew from below-decks blinked in the sun.

Julio worked his way through the crowd of men to stand beside Able Seaman Jamaica Ross and his buddy, Ordinary Seaman Rum Stewart. Jamaica grinned down at him. "Looking smart, my man," he said in the singsong lilt Julio loved.

Julio's heart swelled. He puffed out his chest. "Thanks!"

But then an all-too-familiar voice growled, "For Pete's sake, get that dog out of here."

Julio's heart fell. Jack growled.

"Give it a rest, Chips," Rum said.

"What kind of crew will the commodore think we are with that stupid dog on board, not to mention a little kid?" O'Brien protested.

Julio frowned. How could anyone say Jack was stupid? Julio clenched both his fists and snapped, "He's a lot smarter than *you!*"

Laughter rippled through the crowd.

Chips O'Brien's blue eyes flashed with anger. He pointed his finger just inches from Julio's face. Julio took one step back. An image of the biggest bully at the orphanage flashed through his mind.

"If I had my way, laddie, you and that dog of yours would—"

The door to the captain's quarters opened. Everyone, even O'Brien, froze. A tall man in a dark, crisp uniform and hat with the emblem of the United States Navy flying proudly above the brim stepped out onto the upper deck. Captain Bayne, Chief Engineer Harrison, and First Mate Bay Harvie followed behind.

Quiet fell upon the assembled men. Even Jack seemed to hold his breath.

The commodore surveyed the seamen of the *Susquehanna*. As with most merchant marine crews, they were a mix of young and old, black and white, Italian, Latino, Irish, Australian, even Russian. Commodore Hodges knew that many

of the men had joined the US Merchant Marine because they were too old, too young, or could not pass the physical requirements for the main military branches. But he also knew, just like President Roosevelt did, that you'd never find a braver crew anywhere.

Commodore Hodges smiled. His silver hair shone in the sun. "Good afternoon, men." He nodded. "And dogs." Everyone relaxed just a little bit, especially Julio.

"I've gathered you all here this afternoon to fill you in on this very important mission we are on. I know most of you have sailed in other convoys carrying important supplies to our troops and allies. Just as I'm sure you know the merchant marine is absolutely vital to the success of our winning this war."

The crew stood a little straighter with pride.

"Now, I know the illustrious *Time* magazine calls these Liberty ships 'ugly ducklings,' but beauty never won a war. Courage wins wars, and you men have that in spades."

"Amen to that," Jamaica said quietly, nodding.

The commodore removed his glasses and

wiped them with a perfectly white handkerchief.

Settling his glasses back on his face, he said, "The assignment of this convoy is to deliver supplies to the Flying Tigers, our men fighting the Japanese in the China-Burma-India Theater."

Julio gasped. The Flying Tigers! How many times had he read about them in Captain Bayne's copies of *Stars and Stripes*? How often had he daydreamed of sitting in the cockpit of that fierce fighter plane, its shark mouth opened wide to tear the enemy apart? A chill ran up his arms. Maybe, just maybe, after they got there . . .

"We will proceed on our course south and then east across the Atlantic and round the Cape of Good Hope."

The maps he'd studied in the radio operator's room flashed in Julio's quick mind.

"Whoa," Julio said. "That's a long way!"

Captain Bayne shot him a warning look.

The commodore smiled. "It is indeed, my young friend."

Julio felt his ears burn. He hadn't realized he'd spoken so loudly.

"From there, we'll skirt the east coast of Africa

and then north to India. As your young shipmate observed, it's a long journey and fraught with many dangers," the commodore said. "There are, of course, packs of German U-boats to contend with, and then we will have to deal with the Japanese fighter planes."

A thick wave of anger surged through the crowd. The Japanese had bombed Pearl Harbor in Hawaii five months before. Julio still couldn't believe the United States had been attacked! As terrible as this war was, he never thought they'd be bombed on their own soil. The thought of the lives lost during the attack still made him sick.

"Have no doubt, these supply trucks and tanks are absolutely crucial to fighting this Japanese menace," the commodore said. Even from this distance, Julio could see the steely determination in the commodore's eyes.

"Over the next few weeks, we will increase our convoy emergency drills, including lifeboat maneuvers and evacuation procedures. Every man on this ship must participate in these drills," Commodore Hodges said.

He smiled. "I look forward to getting to know

all of you, two-footed *and* four-footed, over the next weeks."

Julio grinned and patted Jack's head. He liked this commodore.

Radio Operator Sparky, the only crew member who did not leave his post for the meeting, scurried out from the radio room. Julio could see the tension in Sparky's face as he handed the commodore a piece of paper.

The commodore read the message and handed it to Captain Bayne.

The commodore cleared his throat. "Men, we've just received orders from command to change our course."

Julio frowned. The ships rarely changed course unless danger was close. He gripped the bandana around Jack's neck.

"A large, dangerous storm is in our current path. Winds are blowing steady at seventy miles per hour with gusts of wind clocked at ninety miles per hour."

Julio gasped. Those were hurricane force winds!

"We'll have to head southeast instead of due

east to avoid the storm," the commodore said.

Men looked at each other in alarm.

Forgetting himself, Julio said, "But that's where all the German submarines are." Captain Bayne had told him that just a few days before.

"That's right," Julio heard someone behind him say.

The commodore held up his hand. Everyone fell silent again. "I appreciate your concerns," he said, "but I assure you, we're well protected in this convoy."

"Well protected my hat," Julio heard Chips O'Brien mutter behind him. "We'll be lucky to get out of this alive."

A shiver of fear snaked up Julio's spine.

CHAPTER 4

That afternoon, Jack licked his lips as he watched Spud pile lunch leftovers onto a plate for him. The salty smell of canned meat and the sweet smell of canned green beans made Jack's stomach growl. This wasn't the crew's favorite meal, which was just fine with Jack. More for him!

Just as Spud lifted the plate, a whistle blasted from the ship's bridge twice.

"Lifeboat drill," Stewie called from the storeroom. "Better get going."

The men untied their aprons and headed for the stairs.

Jack barked in alarm. Oh, but he was hungry!

"Sorry, Jack!" Spud called from the stairs.

Jack sighed. He eyed the plate on the edge of the counter. It would be easy enough to serve himself. He barely had to stand on his two back legs to reach the plate of delicious smells. But then his boy would be disappointed in him, and Jack never, ever wanted to disappoint Julio. Besides, he did have a job during the lifeboat drills.

Jack looked longingly at the plate of food, then headed out to find his boy.

The crew hurried to their assigned lifeboats as they always did during the drills. But Jack sensed something different this time. The men didn't joke and talk like they usually did. Jack could see the tension in their faces as they took their life vests. He was puzzled by the sharp scent of fear coming from some of the crew. Did it have something to do with the older man who spoke to them earlier that day? The one who held himself like a pack leader?

Jack trotted to the back of the ship, where

he knew Julio would be waiting for him at their assigned lifeboat. They both had jobs to do!

Sure enough, there his boy stood. He looked worried too. Jack barked out a greeting. *Hey, kiddo!*

The worry left Julio's face when he spotted Jack. "Hey, boy," Julio said, hugging Jack around the neck, something Jack did not especially like. Still, it made his boy happy.

Jack pulled away and nudged the boy's leg impatiently. The sooner they got done, the sooner he could go eat.

Jack waited while Julio went from lifeboat to lifeboat and checked each one for supplies.

Julio listed the items out loud. "Fifteen gallons of water, tins of biscuits, chocolate, dried milk, pemmican, first aid kit, and signal mirror. Check. Check. Check."

Once he finished, it was Jack's turn.

Usually Jack enjoyed his job: checking each boat for rats. Checking for rats was an important job. Rats liked to chew holes in the canvas sail and eat biscuits and chocolate. But today, Jack just wanted to get it done.

When he got to the last boat, he ignored the man with the limp, the man who always smelled angry and just a little afraid of Jack. The one who, worst of all, made his boy afraid.

Jack leaped into the lifeboat and began sniffing from one end to the other.

"Get that mutt off my boat!" the man roared.

"He's just checking for rats, sir, like always," Jack heard Julio explain.

The man rounded on the boy. "Don't talk to me like I'm an idiot, you cheeky boy."

Jack whirled at the menace in the man's voice. The man was close, too close, to his boy. The stink of anger and fear surrounded the man and Julio.

Jack took one, then two steps toward the man. He growled a warning deep in his chest. *Leave my boy alone.*

The man's face turned white, then red. He grabbed an oar and raised it above his head. "Get your dog, boy, or I'll use this on him! Don't think I won't!"

For a split second, Jack cowered. How many times when he lived on the streets had humans

raised their fists, their sticks, and caused pain?

But then he saw his boy's eyes widen with fear. He saw his boy cower.

Jack lunged at the man, his powerful jaws snapping in warning to leave Julio alone.

The man shrieked in fear. He swung hard with his one good leg, kicking Jack in his chest.

Pain shot through Jack's body.

He'd had enough of this puny man. He leaped, his jaws wide.

"Jack, no!" Julio flung himself between the man and Jack. He grabbed Jack, holding tight to the annoying bandana tied around his neck.

"Hey!" Strong arms grabbed Jack and lifted him from the lifeboat. He growled, then relaxed just a bit. He smelled Jamaica, a kind and good friend.

"That—that dog's a menace!" The man called Chips sputtered, pointing the oar. "He could have killed me!"

"Jack never touched you," Julio cried, "but you kicked him!" Jack felt his boy's hand shaking with anger and fear.

"I'll do more than just kick him if he ever

comes near me again," Chips hissed.

Jamaica put his arm around Julio's shoulders and turned him away from O'Brien. "You and Jack best get away from here, little man, and let things cool down."

Jack took one last, long look at the man holding the wooden oar.

He narrowed his eyes and growled.

CHAPTER 5

THURSDAY, MAY 22, 1943
3:52 A.M. LOCAL TIME

J ulio held his breath as Chips O'Brien clutched the thermos Julio had just handed him.

"Took you long enough to bring me something hot to drink," O'Brien snapped.

"Sorry, sir." The word "sir" tasted sour in Julio's mouth. It was the last thing he wanted to call Chips O'Brien after what had happened the day before. It had made Julio feel a little bit better that the other crew had given O'Brien a hard time for kicking Jack. But only a little.

Julio had had enough. Nobody hurt his best friend.

O'Brien glanced at his watch and frowned. "You should have been here half an hour ago. These one-to-five watch shifts are the worst."

"Sorry, sir," Julio said through gritted teeth. His body tensed as O'Brien unscrewed the top of the thermos. He knew he should leave as fast as he could, but he wanted—no, needed—to see what happened next.

O'Brien steadied his cup with his left hand— waves heaved the ship up and down—and tipped the thermos with his right.

Instead of steaming hot tea, a small black rat slid out of the thermos, right onto the seaman's lap.

"Holy mother!" O'Brien screeched in terror, leaping to his feet. He fairly danced trying to scramble away from the rat.

Julio slapped his hand over his mouth, trying not to laugh. Everyone knew Chips O'Brien was afraid of rats.

Crew burst from the crew's quarters. Even in

the dark, Julio could see the looks of alarm on their faces.

"What is it, Chips?" Rum asked as he clambered down the stairs to the main deck. "What did you see?"

Jamaica raced to the stern of the ship and positioned himself at the antiaircraft gun.

Julio's heart stuttered. He hadn't thought about this.

Chips jumped from one foot to the other as the rat scurried in between his feet.

"He's seen a rat," Julio said.

"A *rat*?" Rum whipped his hat from his bald head. "All this ruckus is about a *rat*?"

Third Mate Hollywood joined the group, grinning. "Never heard a sailor scream like a little baby before," he said.

Julio relaxed. He'd done it. He'd gotten back at Chips O'Brien for treating Jack so mean.

Jack barked enthusiastically as he chased the rat across the rain-slicked deck of the ship, underneath the trucks lashed to the forward deck, and up to the midship house.

The door to the captain's quarters swung open.

"What in the blue blazes is all the yelling about out here?"

Captain Bayne stood glaring down at the crew in the rain, his face dark with anger.

Jack pranced over to the captain, the rodent dangling from his jaws, and dropped it proudly at the captain's feet. He looked up at Captain Bayne and wagged his stub of a tail.

Chips O'Brien pointed a shaking finger at Julio. "It's the boy's fault, Captain. He put a rat in my thermos." O'Brien's face was still white with fear.

Captain Bayne's footsteps thundered down the stairs from the midship house. They stopped directly in front of Julio.

"Is that true, Julio?"

Julio glanced up at the captain's weathered face. He liked Captain Bayne. He'd been Julio's captain now for over a year and treated him well. But he had never seen him look this angry.

Julio looked back down at the captain's shoes and shrugged. "It was just a small rat, sir, and Jack did his job. He caught it."

Jack sneezed in agreement.

Captain Bayne pinched the bridge of his nose

and closed his eyes. "The rat," he said, biting down hard on each word, "was *inside* the thermos, Martinez."

Julio gulped. Captain Bayne rarely called him by just his last name. "But, sir, Chips kicked Jack yesterday and hurt him!" Julio explained. "He deserved it!" The captain liked Jack, Julio knew. He was always laughing at Jack's antics and slipping him extra food at dinner. He would not like hearing Jack was kicked.

Captain Bayne bent down, his face just inches from Julio's. "O'Brien was on *watch* duty, Martinez. What," the captain asked in a low voice, "is the most important job on the ship, Martinez?"

"The watch," Julio answered, not looking at the captain.

"That's right. And you distracted a man from his watch, Martinez."

That was four times the captain had called him by his last name. Julio swallowed hard to keep back the tears stinging the corners of his eyes.

The captain straightened up. "You've caused enough trouble." He motioned to Rum and Jamaica.

"Take the boy down to his quarters and lock him up. See that he can't get out."

"But—" Julio couldn't believe this. It was just a rat. And O'Brien was a rat too!

"And take the dog too," the captain added, turning his back to Julio. "I don't want the commodore thinking I run a circus here."

Jamaica placed a hand gently on Julio's back. "Come on, Julio, let's go."

"Listen, Captain, Chips had it coming, the old grouch," Julio heard Hollywood say as they walked away. "He's always picking on the kid and the dog."

"I know that," Captain Bayne said, as Julio disappeared into the crew's quarters. "But I've got bigger concerns. Radar's picked up U-boats in the area. Close." It was the last thing Julio heard the captain say.

CHAPTER 6

THURSDAY, MAY 22, 1943
4:10 A.M. LOCAL TIME

"It's not fair!" Julio said through clenched teeth again. "You know how mean Chips has been to me and to Jack ever since he hired on in Savannah. He had it coming."

Jamaica sighed. He pushed open the door to Julio's quarters, which was really just a closet next to the galley, outfitted with a cot, a chair, and a much-used trunk.

"Fair or not," Jamaica said, "you best not be coming out of here until the captain's cooled down. He was pretty mad."

"But I heard Captain Bayne say there are U-boats in the area," Julio said.

"There are always U-boats in the area," Jamaica said with a shrug.

Julio slumped in defeat on his cot. Jack rested his chin on the boy's knee.

"You're lucky this ship doesn't have a brig," Rum said with a chuckle. "I've served my fair share of time in one, and let me tell you, there's not much worse."

He tipped his hat as they left. "I will say, though, putting a rat in his thermos was brilliant."

Julio listened as the two men pushed something heavy against the door on the other side.

"Hey!" Julio protested. "What are you doing?"

"Sorry, little man," Jamaica replied. "Captain's orders."

The ship rolled and bucked in the storm-tossed sea. Lightning lit the round porthole in the wall just above Julio's bed.

Jack paced a tight circle in the tiny room, whimpering.

Julio pulled the dog to him. "It's okay, Jack. I won't let anything—or anybody—hurt you."

Thunder boomed. "We've been in worse storms."

Jack stiffened in his arms. He cocked his head to one side, listening. Julio could tell by the thrust of Jack's ears and the wrinkle of his brow that he heard something beyond the thunder.

Julio frowned. Why was Jack staring at the floor and growling? He'd never seen his dog do that before.

Jack pulled away and jumped against the wooden door, scratching it with his nails.

"Jack, stop!" Julio said.

Jack barked a high warning bark.

"Hey, Jack, it's—"

Boom!

The ship shuttered. The blast tossed Julio like a rag doll from his cot. The porthole glass shattered. His ears popped open and closed, then opened again. Waves sent seawater pouring through the porthole and swirling around Julio's and Jack's feet.

Jack barked over and over and over. A siren shrieked from the main deck above.

Julio scrambled to his feet. "We've been hit, Jack! We've got to get out!"

Julio pushed against the door with all his might. It barely budged.

More sirens sounded in the engine room below. Another blast shook the ship. The *Susquehanna* listed to one side.

Julio pushed harder. "It's too big, whatever it is," he said. His heart hammered in his chest.

Julio beat on the door with his fists. "Help!" he shouted. "Help! Help!"

Jack barked and howled.

Nothing.

CHAPTER 7

Jack panted with fear. The water was getting deeper. He could smell smoke in the engine room below. The screams he'd heard earlier had stopped. But on the main deck above, he could feel the chaos. Perhaps it was a good thing his boy, with his puny ears, was ignorant of those things, Jack thought.

Because Julio was scared. More frightened than Jack had ever smelled. It was Jack's opinion that, on the whole, humans were not particularly brave animals. And who could blame them?

Their teeth were small, they had no fur, and their noses were, from what Jack could tell, basically useless. But his boy was different. Even when he was frightened, he kept his head about him. Julio never gave up. Jack loved this about his boy's heart.

Jack watched as Julio pushed and twisted, trying to make himself as small as possible to squeeze through the opening of the door. It was no use.

Julio grabbed the trunk at the foot of their bed. He gathered his legs beneath him and pushed the trunk across the tiny room. Jack barked encouragement.

The trunk slammed against the door, knocking Julio off his feet.

Just as Jack knew he would, Julio did not give up. Still, no matter how hard he tried, his boy could not squeeze through.

The water grew deeper. An explosion below shook the boat.

The smell of smoke and panic filled the room.

Jack leaped up onto the trunk and nudged Julio aside. Jack had squeezed through some very small spaces on land and on the ship in search of food and rats.

He pushed and wiggled. His wide chest and shoulders scraped hard against the doorjamb. Pain shot across his shoulder, but like Julio, he never gave up.

Finally, his shoulders pushed free of the tight space; the rest of him quickly followed.

Julio cheered and sobbed. "Good boy, Jack! Go get help!"

Jack shook himself. A quick sniff told him everything he needed to know: everyone in the midship quarters and galley were gone. A fire from one of the five cargo holds below burned its way upward. The sharp smell of smoke burned his nose; he felt the heat of the fire through his paws. There was no time to search for help.

In his powerful jaws, Jack grabbed the metal leg of the table blocking the door. He shifted his weight onto his haunches and pulled with every bit of strength he had.

His boy peered through the opening. His eyes gleamed with hope when he saw Jack.

"I'll push with my legs while you pull, Jack."

Jack barked. *Good boy!*

"Okay, Jack, pull!"

Jack pulled; Julio pushed.

The table moved, but not enough.

The heat from the growing fire below burned Jack's feet.

"Again!" Julio cried.

Jack pulled with all his might.

Jack pulled so hard on the table leg, he felt a sharp pain in one tooth.

The ship lurched to one side.

The table slid across the floor.

Julio was free! Jack yipped.

Julio squeezed through the opening, stumbling out to the other side. He threw his arms around Jack and buried his wet face in the dog's neck.

The smell of smoke grew even stronger.

Jack gave his boy a quick lick on the side of his face and a hard nudge that said, *Enough of that, we have to go!*

Julio unwound his arms from Jack's shoulders. Bright-red blood smeared Julio's shirt.

"Jack, you're hurt!"

Jack whimpered, but not from pain. He could hear it coming, that high, thin whine. The ship was already terribly damaged. Jack knew from the smells that men were dead. He could hear the chaos on the main deck above.

Jack felt the sea vibrate as the torpedo tore through the water. How could he protect his boy from this?

Another explosion rocked the *Susquehanna*. The lights in the cabin went out. Utter and complete darkness enveloped them.

Julio whimpered. Jack was the only one who knew that the boy was afraid of the dark, that he always slept with his door partly open for the comfort of the lights from the galley.

Gently, Jack took the boy's wrist in his mouth and led him past the galley, down the hallway past the other crew's bunkrooms, past the dining room, and to the steep metal stairs that led to the main deck above.

Julio felt the stairs with his free hand.

"We have to get to our lifeboat, Jack," Julio said as he clamored up the stairs.

Jack watched from the bottom of the stairs. There was one more thing he needed to do before he followed his boy up to the deck above.

Stay, he barked to his boy. *Wait for me.*

Jack raced back to the galley. He sniffed quickly around, following a scent he normally ignored.

There, huddled under an overturned crate of oranges, was the cat. The fat, lazy, useless cat.

I can't believe I'm doing this, Jack thought.

He picked the cat up by the scruff of the neck.

The cat yowled in protest, but not too strongly.

Jack trotted back down to the stairway, the cat swinging back and forth, and finally, up the stairs. He knew his boy would be worried, waiting for him up there.

He dropped the cat onto the deck none too gently. *You're on your own, cat.*

Jack sniffed all around the top of the stairs, searching for his boy's familiar scent. Julio was not waiting for him like Jack had told him to.

His boy was gone.

The dog's heart raced with panic. Flames licked through the cargo hold. The smell of fear and death and disaster filled his nose. Jack shook with fear. Never had he felt so alone.

Jack caught the scent of someone he knew:

Spud Campbell, his buddy in the ship's galley. Julio helped Spud in the kitchen and gave Jack special treats when he caught rats.

Jack ran over to Spud. He barked his questions. *Where is Julio? Is he hurt?*

Spud looked through Jack as if he were a ghost and hurried away.

Jack's heart fell. How would he ever find Julio?

Then he heard it: "Jack! Jack!" The voice of his boy!

Jack raced across the ship, following the direction of the voice. Where was he?

He leaped onto the side of an overturned supply truck to get a better view. The smoke had thickened, making it impossible to see.

Jack barked desperately.

He heard an answering cry. "Jack, where are you?"

His boy was alive!

Flames shot up through the largest of the supply hatches.

Here! Jack barked. *Here! Here!*

CHAPTER 8

THURSDAY, MAY 22, 1943
5:15 A.M. LOCAL TIME

Julio heard a familiar bark.

"Jack!" he cried. "Where are you?"

He heard a splash.

Julio ran to the starboard side. A hole big enough to drive a supply truck through had been blown into the side, exactly where the engine room was. Water poured into the ship.

In the sea below, a lifeboat full of crew rowed frantically away from the *Susquehanna*.

"Hey!" Julio called down, waving his arms. "Hey! Come back!" He couldn't believe they were leaving him behind. Just like he'd been left behind at the orphanage.

The bark came again.

"Jack!" Julio screamed as loud as he could. "Over here, Jack!"

Out of the smoke, Julio saw the most wonderful sight: Jack racing toward him. Jack leaped into the boy's arms, whimpering and yipping with happiness. Julio held on to the dog like a lifeline.

The ship's whistle blasted the distress signal again.

"Come on, Jack," Julio said. They raced to the left side of the boat, which tilted lower than the right side. One lifeboat hung from its mooring in tatters; the other was still in one piece.

Julio hadn't lowered a lifeboat during their training: everybody said he was too small to handle it on his own. But he had watched closely every time they'd had a drill and memorized how every pulley and cable worked. He liked to daydream about being the only one who could operate the lifeboat, being the one who lowered the lifeboat to the sea, saving everyone on board. They'd be astounded by his skill and his strength. They'd recommend him for a special medal.

He never imagined it would actually happen.

A large wave slammed into the side of the ship, knocking Julio to his knees.

The smell of smoke grew stronger. Jack barked frantically.

"Let's go, Jack!" Julio jumped into the boat, Jack right behind him.

Julio unhooked the cable's anchors, then fed the cable through the pulley to lower the boat.

Or at least that was what should happen.

Only the front end of the boat lowered toward the sea.

Jack barked. Julio looked behind him. The back of the lifeboat still hung high in the air. Normally, two people would lower the boat to the water.

"Crud!" Julio said. "Why didn't I think of that?" He ran to the back of the boat, lowered that end, and then ran back to the front. Back and forth, back and forth Julio went, lowering each end a little at a time.

The muscles in Julio's arms quivered. He looked from their boat to the ocean surface below.

"If we can get close enough," he said to Jack,

"I'll cut the ropes with my knife."

Julio fed the rope through the pulley, one end and then the other.

One foot down. Three feet, then four feet down. Julio, Jack, and the lifeboat slid slowly down the side of the *Susquehanna*.

Suddenly, a wave slapped the lifeboat, hard. Julio staggered to keep his balance. He loosened his grip on the ropes. The ropes raced upward, burning his palms.

"No!" Julio cried.

Smack! The lifeboat slammed onto the surface, almost throwing boy and dog into the ocean.

Julio scrambled to the wooden beam running the width of the boat. He grabbed an oar and rowed desperately to get away from the ship. No matter how hard he rowed, though, the waves and the current kept driving the lifeboat back toward the ship. Fear raced through Julio. He knew that if he got too close to the sinking ship, it could suck the lifeboat down with it.

Suddenly, the fire roared to life. Flames towered mast-high above the ship's bridge.

Julio heard a scream.

CHAPTER 9

Splash!

Something fell from the ship into the sea.

Not five feet from the lifeboat, Julio saw the terrified face of his friend Jamaica.

"Over here!" Julio called, waving his arms.

Jamaica swam with all the strength he had to get away from the suction of the sinking *Susquehanna.* Even in heavy waves, his strokes were strong and sure.

Julio held his oar out for his friend to grab on to, and he pulled him up and over into the boat.

Jamaica lay on the bottom panting. Julio could see that his friend's pants had been burned almost completely off, and his hands were burned too.

Jack licked the man's face over and over.

Jamaica sat up and looked at the ship with wide eyes. Then he blinked and said, "We must get as far away from the ship as we can, man. She's going down fast."

Before Julio could answer, Jamaica grabbed an oar. He sat on the other side of the beam and started rowing. Julio worked hard to match Jamaica's strokes. Soon, they were several yards clear of the sinking *Susquehanna*. They stopped rowing and looked back at the ship that had been their home. The huge steel ship that had always seemed so indestructible to Julio lay on its side. The proud main mast smoldered. Smoke billowed from the prow as the back of the ship sank into the sea.

"I can't believe it," Julio said.

"Believe it." Jamaica sighed. "We're on our own now."

"Won't someone know we were torpedoed and

come looking for us?" Surely Sparky, the radio operator, had gotten a message out. Any second a ship from the convoy would spot them and they'd be saved.

Jamaica shook his head. "The bridge and the engine room were the first things hit."

"I stayed on ship blowing the distress signal as long as I could," he continued, "but who's around to hear it?"

"But the other ships in the convoy—"

"Sank or ran off," Jamaica said, cutting him off. "Ships in a convoy aren't allowed to go back to look for survivors, and rescue boats only have fifteen minutes to search the waters around the ship. Otherwise, they'd get picked off by the U-boats too."

Julio felt like one of those torpedoes had hit him in the gut.

Jamaica pulled two life vests from beneath the bench. "Best put this on," he said, tossing a vest to Julio.

Jack barked a high, excited bark. He ran to the front of the lifeboat, looked back at Julio and

Jamaica, and barked again.

Then they heard it. Out of the early dawn mist came a cry. "Help! Help me!"

"Someone's over there!"

With a burst of energy, Julio and Jamaica grabbed their oars and rowed in the direction of the cries.

"There!" Julio said, pointing. "I see him!"

Clinging to a barrel of cooking oil was Chief Cook Stewie.

Jamaica extended his oar. "Here, grab on!" Slowly, he pulled the cook into the boat.

"Oh, are you a sight for sore eyes," Stewie gasped. "I thought I was a goner for sure."

"Have you seen anyone else?" Jamaica asked.

Stewie shook his head.

"We've got to keep looking," Julio said. "There have to be more of the crew out here that need us."

They rowed through the debris and floating boxes of supplies, looking for survivors. No one spoke. They listened for more cries of help. An eerie quiet enveloped them as surely as the thickening fog.

"Maybe we're all what's left," Stewie said.

"I know for sure I'm the only one who made it out from the bridge," Jamaica said in a flat voice.

Jack barked.

"Quiet," Jamaica ordered.

Jack moved to the front of the lifeboat. He strained so far out over the prow of the boat, Julio worried he'd fall into the water. Jack's ears moved one way and then the other. He barked again, staring intently into the fog.

"Poor dog's hallucinating," Stewie said.

"Jack can hear a thousand times better than we can," Julio said. "His ears don't lie."

Still, they couldn't hear anything except the cry of seabirds and the slap of the waves against the lifeboat.

Jack barked again, his paws dancing on the rail of the boat.

Julio jumped to his feet. "I see someone over there!" He hoped with everything he had it was Captain Bayne. The captain would know what to do. The captain would make everything okay.

Quickly, they rowed over to the man clinging

to a wooden pallet. Wet hair was plastered across his face, but he did have a beard like Captain Bayne. Julio's heart leaped with hope.

But when they heaved the man into the life-boat, it was not Captain Bayne. It was Chips O'Brien.

CHAPTER 10

Jack studied the man they'd just pulled into the lifeboat: the bad man who had kicked him, who had threatened his boy. Oh, he didn't look quite the same, all bedraggled by the sea, but he smelled the same. His nose didn't lie.

Jack narrowed his eyes and glared at the man. *I'll be watching you every minute.* He put his body between the man and his boy. Jack saw a flash of fear in the man's eyes.

The four humans rowed the lifeboat through boxes and bins and debris floating on the sea.

Sea birds squawked and squabbled over piles of powdered eggs and dried potatoes floating on the surface. Jack had missed breakfast, and he was hungry! He barked and lunged at the birds, driving them away from the food.

The men steered the lifeboat alongside the floating food. Jack lunged for a mouthful of eggs. He slipped halfway out of the boat.

"Jack!" his boy cried. He grabbed Jack around his middle and dragged him back into the boat. The boat tipped wildly from one side to the other, almost tossing Stewie into the pile of eggs.

"That dog will be the death of us!" the bad man, Chips O'Brien, snapped.

Jack licked Julio's face in thanks. How embarrassing that his boy had had to rescue him and he didn't have a bite of food to show for it.

"Jack, you've got to be more careful," his boy whispered in his ears. Jack could smell the thick scent of fear on his boy's skin. He ducked his head in shame.

The men pulled more boxes and bins from the ocean. Jack thoroughly sniffed every one of them in hopes of food.

One tub held plastic dishes that still smelled faintly of food. Another crate held wool blankets, the kind he and Julio snuggled beneath in their room on the ship.

Then he smelled it again: food! Jack leaped to his feet and searched the air for the smell. There, floating just a few feet away, a plastic tub with a warm, sweet smell inside.

Jack looked back at Julio, wagging his stubby tail. *Food! I found food!* he yipped.

Jamaica grabbed the tub and plopped it onto the bench. Jack quivered in anticipation as his friend pried open the lid. Oh, it smelled so good!

It was yellow. It was creamy. It was a tub full of butter.

Jack's mouth watered at the smell. *Oh please, oh please,* he whined.

"Don't let that dog drool all over the butter," O'Brien said. He reached out to push Jack away. Jack lifted his lip in warning.

"Let's store it with the other food we have on the boat," Stewie said. "Who knows what we might use it for."

Jack's ears sank with disappointment as the

cook snapped the lid back on the beautiful butter.

"Wait," his boy said. "Jack found it. It's only fair he gets a little."

Jack's ears snapped back up. He looked hopefully from his boy to the cook.

Stewie shrugged. "Fair's fair." The cook scooped a small mound of butter with the metal spoon he always kept in his pants pocket and handed it to Julio.

"Here you go, Jack." Julio scraped the butter off the spoon and held out his fingers for Jack to lick.

Jack licked the butter greedily. *Oh, it was so sweet! It was so milky! It was—*

Jack stopped. He felt something large, something metal beneath the water coming toward them. Jack could feel the vibration of this underwater ship through the bottom of the lifeboat. It was keeping itself hidden not because it was avoiding them, but—Jack knew as certainly as he knew the scent of his boy—because it was hunting them.

CHAPTER 11

Suddenly, Jack stopped licking. The hair stood up on the dog's neck and back as he stared with alarm into the fog.

"What is it, Jack?" At first Julio didn't see anything. And then, like something out of a nightmare, he saw the eye of a periscope peering at them like the eye of a monster.

"Look," Julio said, just above a whisper. "Look!" he said, louder.

The men turned as one, setting the boat to rocking. They all watched, speechless, as the periscope stopped barely fifty feet from the life-boat.

Slowly, the submarine rose to the surface, water sheeting from its sides.

A deep growl rumbled in Jack's chest.

Hope lifted Julio's heart. Could it be someone coming to rescue them?

The hair rose higher on Jack's neck and along his spine.

Sunlight broke through the thick fog, glinting off the sub's deck and conning tower.

Julio's blood froze at the sight of the symbol painted on the side of the tower: on one side the image of a fierce boar with deadly tusks, on the other side, the German flag. This was no Allied sub, it was a German U-boat.

"Holy mother," Stewie whimpered.

They heard a clank and the squeal of metal turning on metal.

To their horror, the door to the main hatch opened.

A tall man in a dark uniform climbed easily onto the deck of the submarine. His blond hair was carefully combed, his white shirt immaculate.

The submachine gun dangling from one hand looked deadly.

He surveyed the ragtag group in the lifeboat as cigarette smoke drifted from his nostrils.

The crew remained completely silent. All except Jack, who continued to growl deep in his chest.

The man flicked his cigarette into the sea. "I am Commander Nicolai Clausen," he said. "Who is the captain here?" Julio started in surprise: the man spoke almost perfect English!

"The captain is not in our lifeboat," Jamaica answered.

Clausen gestured with the submachine gun toward the sinking *Susquehanna*. "He remains on board?"

Julio saw Jamaica's face tighten. "He was on the bridge when the first torpedo hit."

Julio gasped. The other crew members swore under their breath.

"What was your ship's name and what was she carrying?" the commander asked.

No one answered. Commander Clausen tapped the stock of the gun with his finger. "It is

best if you respond," he said coldly.

Chips O'Brien cleared his voice. "She was the *Susquehanna*, and we were carrying supply trucks and general cargo."

Julio shot a look at O'Brien. Why was he giving this guy information? The commander was the enemy, after all.

The commander nodded. "And where were you taking the trucks and supplies?"

Without missing a beat, O'Brien answered, "The coast near Freetown, Africa."

Clausen studied the widening oil slick from the *Susquehanna* through his binoculars. "She had a great deal of fuel for such a short journey."

Julio gulped. Jack growled.

"We were also delivering supplies to allies near Spain," Jamaica said, smooth as silk.

Clausen shook his head and laughed. Then his face hardened. "You take me for a fool?" he snapped.

Julio's knees shook. They would all likely be shot now.

Jack stood up tall, almost on his tiptoes, and growled loudly.

The commander pointed his gun at the dog.

"No!" Julio cried, throwing his arms around his dog. "Don't shoot him!" Julio slipped his hand into his pocket and curled his fingers around his pocketknife.

The commander frowned. "Why would I shoot such a fine dog?" He cocked his head to one side.

"I had a boxer as a young boy," the commander continued. "He was a good dog. Very brave. Very loyal."

Julio nodded. "Yes, sir, he is."

Julio could not believe he was in a lifeboat far out in the Atlantic Ocean discussing dogs with a German U-boat commander.

Someone called from inside the submarine.

The commander glanced at his watch. "Do you need supplies before we go? Water? Food?"

"We're not taking anything from a Nazi," Stewie said, spitting into the water. "We'd rather die."

The commander shrugged. "And die you might," he said. He motioned to someone inside the sub. An arm rose through the hatch, handing up a box and a small bag. He stuffed them into a canvas bag. With surprising accuracy, he tossed it the toward the lifeboat.

Jack leaped into the air and grabbed the bag.

The commander laughed. "Good dog!" he called.

Jack dropped the bag at Julio's feet.

"Good luck to you," Commander Clausen called as he descended back into the U-boat. "I am sorry I had to sink your ship, but alas, this is war." He touched the brim of his hat and disappeared. The hatch banged closed behind him.

Julio watched in amazement as the U-boat backed slowly away and then sank like a dream, below the surface.

Jack pawed at the canvas bag, breaking the spell.

"Watch it," Jamaica said, "there might be a bomb in there!"

CHAPTER 12

Julio pulled Jack away. Everyone scrambled as far back as they could get from the bag. The lifeboat rocked and dipped, almost throwing Julio out of the boat.

"Hey," Chips cried. "Watch what you're doing!" He picked up the canvas bag. "You fools are a lot more likely to kill us than the Germans."

Chips opened the bag and reached in. Julio held his breath as he pulled out several boxes.

He held up a large block. "Cheese." Jack barked and wagged his stump of a tail.

"Limes." Julio wasn't a big fan of limes. Still, he knew they would need the vitamin C they held so they wouldn't get scurvy. Surely, though, they wouldn't be lost at sea that long.

Chips smiled as he held a small tin aloft. "Chocolate." Jamaica and Julio cheered.

Lastly, he pulled another, larger, wax-sealed tin from the bag.

Chips squinted at the box. "Anyone read German?"

"I do," Stewie answered. He shrugged at the surprised looks on the crew's faces. "Well, just a little. When I was a kid, our next-door neighbor was German. She taught me a few words."

He took the tin from O'Brien. He frowned as he sounded out the words. *"Salbe. Notfall. Bandagen. Verbandkasten."*

His face lit up. "It's a first aid kit! They've given us a first aid kit!"

"Could be useful," Chips O'Brien said. "Put that in a safe place."

"Drinking water would have been better," Jamaica grumbled.

"We have water," Julio said. That had been

one of his jobs for the lifeboat drills: to make sure each boat had fifteen gallons of drinking water. He scuttled to the rear of the boat and unscrewed a floorplate. Inside was a red fifteen-gallon container of water. He unscrewed another floorplate and pulled it off. "And," he said, smiling, "we have more food."

"Good thing we have a cook on board," Jamaica said with a wan smile. "We'll dine like officers." No one laughed except Stewie. Everyone was thinking about Captain Bayne.

"Was the captain really on the bridge when the torpedo hit?" Julio asked Jamaica. He hoped with all his heart that Jamaica had been lying to the U-boat commander.

Jamaica sighed. "They were all up in the bridge house—Captain Bayne, First Mate Harvie, Chief Engineer Harrison, even Commodore Hodges—plotting a new course to avoid the storm like the big brass told them to."

Jamaica took a deep breath. "I had just started talking with Deck Engineer Casarez when the first torpedo hit."

Everyone was quiet, remembering that terrible

moment. *Could it really have only been a couple of hours ago?* Julio thought. It felt like years.

"For some reason, I ran up to the bridge. When I got there, the whole thing was destroyed . . . and everyone in it."

Julio remembered the distress signal whistle blasts. "Is that when you started blowing the ship's whistle?"

Jamaica nodded. "I saw right away that the radio room—and Sparky—were gone too. Figured I better start letting the other ships know we were in trouble."

No one said anything for a long while.

Finally, Stewie said, "That's it then. We're the only survivors."

Julio remembered the other lifeboat, the one that had left him and Jack behind. "No, there was another lifeboat that I saw before I lowered mine. It was pretty full."

"Which direction did they go?" Chips asked Julio.

Julio shook his head. "I don't know. They launched from the other side of the ship. I didn't see them after that."

"A lot of good that does us," O'Brien grumbled. "You should have kept your eye on them."

It was everything Julio could do not to scream, "Where were you when I was trying to lower a twenty-eight-foot lifeboat by myself!"

Jamaica frowned. "I think the boy had his hands full, O'Brien."

"Well, he could have watched while you two lowered the lifeboat," O'Brien said, nodding at Stewie.

"O'Brien, man," Jamaica said. "Julio lowered that lifeboat alone. Well, except for Jack."

"But you were on the lifeboat, too, when you fished me out of the drink," Stewie said.

"I was," Jamaica said. "But Julio fished *me* out of the drink."

The crew looked at Julio, astonished. Even O'Brien.

Stewie shook his head. "Now isn't that something?"

Jack barked a warning bark. He looked to the north, following something upward with his eyes.

"Is that mutt going to bark at every little—" O'Brien's latest tirade was cut short by a red flash in the distance.

"It's an emergency flare!" Julio cried. "It must be the other lifeboat!"

Everyone scrambled to grab an oar and started rowing.

The rope burns on Julio's hands screamed in pain; his head swam and his empty stomach growled, but they had to follow that flare!

Something, though, prickled in the back of Julio's mind. Flares. Had he seen flare guns on the lifeboats during the last drill? After all, that had been his job during emergency drills: to check supplies on the lifeboats. Every boat had food, water, a small sail, a mast, a bucket, and a signal mirror. But this time, no flare guns.

Then Julio remembered. He stopped rowing. Disappointment filled his empty stomach.

"There aren't flare guns on our lifeboats," Julio stated flatly.

Stewie looked at him with disbelief. "Why not?"

Julio sighed. "Because Captain Bayne forgot to get them in Savannah." Julio's ears burned at the memory of his hero, the captain, making a mistake. "He said we'd get more as soon as we got to our first port."

Stewie looked at Jamaica, and they both looked at Chips.

"Then whose flare was that?" Stewie asked.

"Could have been a German U-boat in trouble," O'Brien said with a shrug. "Or one trying to lure in a rescue boat. They do those sorts of things. Still," he said, "we should row in that direction, just in case."

In case of what, Julio wondered. He studied the Irishman while he rowed. Why did O'Brien seem to know so much about these things? And he certainly hadn't seemed that afraid of the U-boat commander.

Was he a spy? A traitor? Just who was Chips O'Brien?

CHAPTER 13

Jack lay panting in the searing afternoon sun. He couldn't remember the last time he'd eaten or had a cool drink of water. And to make matters worse, there was no shade in the open lifeboat.

His head pounded and his tongue felt too big for his mouth. Boy oh boy, what he wouldn't give to snooze away in the ship's bridge where it was always nice and cool. And even better, sometimes Captain Bayne gave him treats.

Jack crawled beneath the wooden bench

where Julio sat rowing. At least there, his head was in the shade.

Jack watched the men as they rowed hour after hour. He'd lived on the ship with them for over a year. He'd felt their anger, heard their laughter, listened to their fears and longings. He could read them by the slumped shoulders, the groans as they pulled on the oars, the worried looks at the endless sea. They were scared, they were exhausted, they were determined. He could read them almost as well as he could read his boy.

All except that man O'Brien.

The sound of the oars in the water stopped.

"I can't row another stroke without some water and food," Jack heard Stewie say.

Jamaica muttered in agreement.

O'Brien unscrewed the top of the water jug. The sweet smell of fresh water filled Jack's nose. He scrambled to his feet and watched as O'Brien filled cups with delicious water.

Jack's feet danced with excitement.

He watched his boy raise the cup to his lips and take a long drink. Then, just as Jack knew he would, Julio lowered the cup for Jack.

"Here you go, boy."

Jack pinned his ears back in thanks.

"Hey!" Chips O'Brien grabbed the cup from Julio's hand. "We don't have enough water to be giving it to that dog." He glared at Julio and Jack.

Jack couldn't believe it! One minute he was about to take a drink of water and the next, it was snatched right out from under his nose!

His body tensed; his eyes narrowed. The man was a rat, and Jack knew just how to deal with rats.

Julio grabbed the cup right back. In a voice Jack had rarely heard his soft-spoken boy use, he said, "They're my rations, not yours!"

"You're just a boy," the man spat. "You're not old enough to make these kinds of decisions."

Jack could feel the anger in Julio, and just a whiff of fear. He put himself between his boy and the man.

Without taking his eyes from the man, Julio filled the cup with water and placed it in front of Jack.

Jack was so proud of his boy. He showed that man who's top dog!

Then, wonder of wonders, Jamaica opened the box of cheese the tall man from the submarine had given them.

Oh, had anything ever smelled so delicious? Jack whimpered longingly. He watched with laser focus as Jamaica sliced pieces of cheese and handed them around. His stomach clenched and he licked his lips in anticipation as Julio took his piece.

Again, just as Jack knew he would, Julio broke the piece of cheese in half. It took all of Jack's self-control to take the cheese gently from his boy's fingers.

Chips O'Brien shook his head. "Don't come crying to me when you're hungry."

Jack felt his boy tense. "I always share with Jack," he said.

Chips shrugged. "Your funeral."

"What a thing to say!" Stewie protested.

Jack smelled anger pouring from Jamaica. He felt the tension that had been building in the boat all day coming to a dangerous head.

One of his jobs on the ship had been to keep the men happy. Jack grabbed a wet wool blanket that had been drying in the sun. He had no idea what to do with it, but he had to work with what he had. He dragged it over to Chips and dropped it at his feet. He stepped back and wagged his stub of a tail.

Chips frowned. "What's this dog doing?"

Jamaica laughed. "I think Jack's trying to tell you not to be such a wet blanket, man."

Stewie hooted with laughter. "Is that it, Jack old boy?"

Jack sneezed twice. Jack wasn't sure why, but everyone enjoyed it when he sneezed.

The castaways laughed and laughed. Even O'Brien managed a half smile.

Jack felt the tension melt away. He curled up again beneath his boy's legs and sighed. He had done his job. He was a good dog.

CHAPTER 14

Julio groaned. His first night spent on the lifeboat had been a long one.

Even though the lifeboat was twenty-eight-feet long, it still felt like they were sardines in a can when they tried to sleep. He'd used one of the wool blankets as a cushion between him and the wooden ribs sticking up from the bottom of the boat, but it didn't do much good. And to make matters worse, everyone snored, even Jack. So instead, he'd watched the stars as he rubbed his thumb over and over his father's compass in his pocket.

"Oh, sweet Mary," Julio heard Stewie groan. "What I wouldn't give for my old, ratty mattress on the ship."

"Me too," Jamaica agreed. "And your biscuits and gravy for breakfast!"

Julio snapped his fingers. "We don't have gravy, but we do have biscuits and butter!" He pulled the food container from the storage bin and grabbed the package of biscuits.

"There's powdered milk too," he reminded them. "And pemmican."

"I'll eat my hat before I'll eat pemmican," Stewie said.

Julio had never eaten pemmican, but it was legendary for its terrible taste.

"You'd be surprised what you'll eat when you have to," O'Brien said grimly.

Julio shivered. O'Brien sounded like he spoke from experience. Once again, Julio wondered just what that experience was.

The wind picked up as the crew ate their breakfast. Julio expected Chips to say something when he gave Jack half his rations, but he only glared.

"Wind's blowing steady and strong," Chips said. "We'll raise the sail and take advantage of it."

"Shouldn't we stay close to where the *Susquehanna* sank?" Stewie asked.

"I don't think we're anywhere near where it went down," Julio said.

Stewie frowned. "How do you know?"

Julio pointed to the sky. "The star patterns. They've changed." He'd been fascinated in the books he'd read in the library about navigating by the stars.

Chips nodded. "I noticed it last night too. Between the currents and the waves, we're far from where we went down."

"So now what do we do?" Jamaica asked.

"Set a course," Chips said.

"To where?"

"Land," Chips answered.

The men looked from one to another and then to what surrounded them in every direction: endless sea. So endless it seemed impossible that land, the very idea of land, existed.

"The problem is, we don't know what our last

known location was," Chips said with a shrug.

A map flashed in Julio's mind. The map up on the bridge Captain Bayne had shown him just hours before Julio had gotten into trouble. Just hours before *his* last known location had exploded.

"I think I know," Julio said. "I saw the navigation chart Captain Bayne was using to mark our route. He showed me the *X* that marked where we were."

"How long was that before the U-boat attacked?" Jamaica asked.

"Only three, maybe four hours."

Jamaica looked intently at the boy. "Julio, do you remember what coast we were nearest?"

Julio nodded. "South America. Captain Bayne said we were about three hundred miles northeast of Brazil."

"The *Susquehanna* travels at about eleven miles per hour," Jamaica said. "So that means we'd gone another forty to fifty miles when we got torpedoed."

"Then that's where we need to go," Julio said. "Southwest, back to South America."

Chips gazed out over the Atlantic. "That's

over three hundred and fifty miles southwest," he pointed out. "*If* we plan to trust the boy's memory, that is."

Julio felt his ears burn with anger.

"I trust his memory more than I trust mine," Jamaica said. "Besides, do you have a better idea of where we are?"

"Yeah," Julio said, glaring at Chips. "What *is* your idea?" *Especially if you're a spy,* Julio thought.

Everyone watched the Irishman, waiting for his answer. Finally, Chips shrugged. "Southwest it is."

"But how do we even know which way is southwest?" Stewie said. "I mean, we know the sun sets in the west, but how do we know which way is south?" Stewie looked at the endless horizon.

Julio pulled his father's compass out of his pocket. "This will help," he said, holding it up.

Jamaica grinned. "Brilliant!"

"Do you really think we can row over three hundred miles?" Stewie asked, wide-eyed.

"I think we can," Julio said. "Other people have survived in a lifeboat, sometimes for a long time." After all, he'd read *Robinson Crusoe* twice. Not quite the same, but still.

Everyone looked doubtful. Except Jack, that is.

"If we take turns rowing, I bet we can cover at least twenty miles a day," Julio said.

"That would take us over twenty-two days," Stewie said. "We only have enough food and water for ten days!"

"But today we have a steady wind," Jamaica pointed out. "If we get the sail up, we could cover a lot more than twenty miles."

"But what if a search boat comes looking for us?" Stewie said.

"Stewie, can't you get it through that thick head of yours? No one is looking for us!" Chips snapped.

Anger filled the lifeboat.

Julio felt the wind push at his back. His hands clenched in frustration. They didn't have time to argue. They had to get the sail up while the wind held!

Julio began to untie the canvas sail. Why, he wondered, did he have to be the one doing this? He was just a kid.

Jamaica touched his shoulder. "I'll help you, my friend."

"Thanks," Julio said, turning his face so Jamaica wouldn't see his tears.

Then he gasped. For the first time, he saw the angry red burns on Jamaica's arms and legs. They looked infected.

Jamaica saw Julio's stricken face. He rolled his shirt sleeves down to cover the burns. "It'll be all right, man," he said.

Finally, Stewie shrugged. "Well, I guess I don't have anything better to do."

"Right," Jamaica said. "Didn't the recruiter tell us being a merchant marine meant adventure and seeing foreign lands?" Everyone laughed, even Stewie.

"And didn't the commodore say we have courage in spades?" Julio said.

At the mention of the commodore, the men grew silent.

Stewie and Chips pulled the mast up tall and straight, then ran the sail up the guy lines. The sail shivered, then filled with wind.

Julio smiled with relief. Finally they were working together.

"Okay, boy," Chips O'Brien called above the hum of the wind in the lines. "Show us the way to go."

Julio moved the compass this way and that until the needle pointed, steady and true.

"That way," Julio said, pointing toward the western horizon.

CHAPTER 15

Jack crouched in the bottom of the lifeboat. It seemed like the boat had been bouncing and skipping over the choppy sea for hours. He'd rarely felt seasick on ships before, and he'd been in his share of storms. But in the lifeboat, there wasn't much between him and the waves. The biscuit he'd shared with Julio squirmed in his stomach. At least the dark clouds kept the sun from roasting him too, he thought.

Jack watched his boy with concern. Julio sat next to Jamaica and Stewie. Usually the boy was happy and relaxed when he was with Jamaica, but even in this wind, Jack could smell the worry coming from his boy. He needed to comfort him.

Jack forced himself to his feet.

He picked his way carefully over to Julio and Jamaica. Jack tilted his head as he studied Jamaica. He understood why his boy was worried. The wounds on the man's arms and legs were bad. Very bad. Underneath the sharp-smelling liquid Stewie rubbed on Jamaica's wounds, Jack could smell fever, infection. And beneath that, he could smell fear and pain.

Jack felt helpless. He could not chase this bad thing away from his friend; there was nothing he could bring him to make him better. All he could do was stay close and comfort him, the way Jamaica had comforted his boy in the past.

Carefully, so as not to get in anyone's way, he curled up next to Jamaica and lay his head on his friend's shoulder. He felt Jamaica relax just the tiniest bit as he lay a fevered hand on Jack's head.

"Thanks, Jack," he whispered.

For the next hour, Jack lay close to Jamaica. He listened to the man moan with pain and whisper in his fevered dreams. Jack did not know what the man said, but he knew he needed to stay close. He did not leave his side, even when Julio moved to the other end of the boat. He did not leave even when Jamaica's fevered body burned him like the sun overhead.

This was where he was needed.

Later, Jamaica shivered and shook despite the hot sun. "Cold," he mumbled. "So cold."

Jack scrambled to his feet. Finally, words he knew, something he could fix!

He found a wool blanket forgotten in a corner and dragged it back over to Jamaica. As he had done when Julio complained of being cold, he pulled the blanket over the man.

"Thanks, my friend," Jamaica said, with a trace of a smile.

Later, much later, after the sun had slipped into the ocean and the stars studded the sky, Jack kept watch over the crew and the boat.

The man Stewie snored as he slept, slumped against the oars.

Jamaica slept fitfully, and Julio dreamed. Jack

could tell it was a good dream because the boy smiled in his sleep. Oh, how he loved that boy!

Only the man Chips was awake. He sat at the tiller, guiding the boat and keeping watch too. Jack took the measure of the man. He could see the tense set of Chips's shoulders and smell the worry as he studied the clouds on the far horizon.

Jack had to admit, he admired the man's loyalty to the boat. He could tell the man could read the wind almost as well as he could. And he stood his ground, like Jack.

Jack knew the man probably needed his company. The company of someone as steadfast as he. Someone who understood.

But Jack could not forget the other part of the man. The part that yelled at his boy and angered him, frightened him. No one did that to his boy.

With a snort, Jack turned his back on Chips. He curled up next to his dreaming boy and tried to sleep.

But there was a change in the wind. One minute it blew steady from the south, then it quickly switched to the east. The air grew heavy and filled with warning.

Jack sat up and searched the sky. Thunder rumbled deep and menacing in the distance. Lightning lit the sky. In the flash, Jack saw the fear in Chips O'Brien's eyes.

A gust of wind nearly tore the sail from the rigging. Thunder stampeded toward the lifeboat.

Jack moaned and shook. He pressed into Julio's side and burrowed his face in his boy's comforting smell. But there was little comfort to be found as the storm raced across the open water.

CHAPTER 16

Julio woke with a start.

He'd been sleeping curled up in the warmth of Jack, dreaming about someone with dark, strong arms throwing him higher and higher in the air, and then catching him. His heart had soared with joy every time the strong hands caught him and held him, safe.

Jack's whimpers pulled him from his dreams.

He stroked his dog's side. "It's okay, Jack. It's okay." Julio frowned. Jack was the bravest dog he'd ever met. What had scared him?

The answer came seconds later. To the west, lightning lit the sky. With each flash, Julio saw huge, nightmarish walls of dark thunderheads. Even though Jack was terrified of thunderstorms, Julio thought they were exciting. He'd watched lots out over the ocean from the safety of the bridge of the *Susquehanna*.

But now his stomach dropped to his knees. A twenty-eight-foot open lifeboat was no match for a big storm!

Julio scrambled to his feet. The boat plowed bravely through the four-foot waves, wind billowing the sail. The wind rattled the mast's rigging. The waves were manageable, Julio thought, and the wind still filled the sails. The rain was light. Maybe the storm wasn't as bad as it looked.

Chips sat in the back at the tiller, guiding it through the rough seas. Jamaica and Stewie slept in the bottom of the boat. So why did he have this sick feeling like something terrible was about to happen?

Lightning flashed, closer this time. Thunder crashed in the distance. The air felt supercharged with electricity. The hair stood up on the back of Julio's neck.

Julio made his way back to Chips. The Irishman's face was tight with fear.

Julio swallowed. "It's a bad one, isn't it?"

Chips nodded. "'Tis."

Julio could see the tension on the Irishman's face.

Lighting split the sky.

"One Mississippi, two Mississippi, three Mississippi," Julio counted under his breath. He'd been at sea long enough to know how to figure out the closeness of a storm by counting the seconds between the flash of lightning and the sound of thunder.

Boom!

"Thirteen seconds." Quickly, Julio divided by five. His heart stopped. "The storm's barely two and a half miles away," he whispered.

Chips frowned. "Never have liked the number thirteen," he said.

"We're in trouble, aren't we?" Julio asked.

Julio saw Chips clench his jaw tight. "Aye," he said.

Could this be the storm they'd changed course to avoid? Julio wondered.

A gust of wind screamed through the rigging. Rain slashed Julio's face.

"Get your life vest on, lad," Chips ordered. "Make sure Jamaica has his on too."

It had been so hot in the boat, they'd all taken their vests off.

"I've already got it on," Jamaica said, sitting up for the first time that day.

"What in the blue blazes is this?" Stewie called above the wild wind.

As if in answer, lightning turned the night to day; thunder crashed right on top of the boat.

"A storm!" Julio cried. "A bad one! And it's close!"

"Bring me the bucket," Jamaica called hoarsely over the wind.

Julio frowned. "Are you going to be sick?"

Jamaica grimaced. "No. But we'll need everything we can to bail water from the boat."

Stewie hurried to grab the bucket and anything else he could find—bowls, cups, even shoes—to bail.

Julio heard a moan and a low howl. Jack! How could he have forgotten Jack?

He took the dog in his arms. "I'm here, Jack. It'll be okay." He felt the dog shaking hard. Julio took the extra life vest he'd been using as a pillow and threaded Jack's front legs through the arm holes, then buckled it around his chest. Boxers were good at most things, but they were not natural born swimmers. At least the vest would give him a fighting chance if the worst happened.

The choppy waves turned to swells. Julio watched in horror as a huge wave towered above them.

Julio saw the white of Chips's knuckles as he gripped the tiller. He steered the nose of the lifeboat into the wave.

The lifeboat clawed its way up and up the face of the wave. For a second that felt like hours, the boat hung on the lip of the wave.

"Jesus, Mary, and Joseph," Stewie moaned.

Julio knew they stood little chance of surviving if they didn't make it over the top of the wave.

He closed his eyes and squeezed the compass in his pocket tight. "Please, Papa," he whispered.

A gust of wind pushed the lifeboat over the lip; the boat careened down the other side.

Julio nearly fell to his knees with thanks. They'd made it! Surely they had a guardian angel.

But when he opened his eyes, he saw another wave breaking over the nose of the boat.

"Bail!" Stewie screamed.

Julio scooped water with a bowl until he thought his arms would surely fall off. Just then, he saw the supply box full of food slosh past his feet and head for the sea.

"No!" he cried. He lunged across the boat, trying to grab the bin before it made it over the side. An unexpected wave slapped the side of the boat, sending it spinning.

Before he had time to think, Julio was pitched over the side of the lifeboat and into the wild Atlantic Ocean.

CHAPTER 17

SATURDAY, MAY 24, 1943
3:52 A.M. LOCAL TIME

Jack heard his boy scream. He saw a wave grab Julio and pull him into the sea.

No! Jack barked. *No! No! No!*

He sniffed frantically for any scent of Julio, but the salt water sloshing in and out of the boat washed away all traces of his boy.

"Man overboard!" Jack heard O'Brien cry through the wind and rain.

Jamaica and Stewie stopped bailing and rushed to Jack's side.

"Dear lord," Stewie moaned. "Not the boy. He

won't stand a chance."

Then Jack saw it: Julio's dark head bobbing above the waves.

Julio! Jack barked. *Julio!*

A wave crashed on top of his boy, burying him.

Jack's heart froze. Where was he? Where was his boy? He had to go help him, but he was sick and weak from sun and heat.

Stewie tore his shoes from his feet and yanked off his shirt. "I'm going in after him!"

"No!" Chips ordered. "You need to keep bailing!"

Jack felt Stewie hesitate.

Then, miracle of miracles, Julio's head popped up above the waves.

"Help!" he heard his boy cry. "Help!"

That was all it took.

Jack gathered all the strength he had and launched himself from the boat. He barked and struck out for the boy. His front legs beat against the waves as he kicked with his back legs.

Thunder crashed. Waves washed over the dog's head. None of that mattered now. All that mattered was finding Julio.

But where was he? Jack swam one way and then circled back the other. No Julio.

A flash of lightning lit the water.

There! There was his boy! Jack barked.

"Jack!" the boy cried.

Jack swam with all his might, never taking his eyes from Julio.

"I'm coming, Jack!" Julio swam with all his might toward his dog.

Dog and boy locked eyes in the storm-tossed sea.

In seconds that felt like hours, Jack reached his boy. Julio wrapped his arms around Jack's life jacket and held on tight.

"There they are!" Jack felt the lifeboat pull up beside him.

"Grab the oar!" Jack heard O'Brien call to Julio.

Julio grabbed for the oar. A wave knocked it away from his hand. Jack swam behind the boy and pushed him toward the boat.

Julio lunged again, grabbing the oar.

"Hang on, lad!" O'Brien called.

Jack paddled and watched anxiously as his boy

was pulled safely into the boat.

His job was done. His boy was safe.

Suddenly Jack was very tired. He could barely lift his front legs. And he was cold, so cold. For the first time he envied that big black dog he'd met once called a Newfoundland. Such a big, warm coat! *Not the brightest dog,* Jack thought, *but—*

Strong arms plucked Jack from the water. Jack looked up into the face of his enemy.

"I've got him, Julio," Chips O'Brien called over his shoulder.

And then his boy was beside him, stroking him, hugging him, wrapping him in a wet wool blanket.

Jack thumped his bit of a tail and licked his boy's hand in thanks.

Everything was okay now. They were together. Even the Atlantic Ocean would not keep them apart.

The rain lessened, and the sea calmed.

"I think the worst of it's over," Chips said.

Stewie laughed. "Boy howdy, that was a heck of a blow!"

Jamaica eased himself back down onto his

blankets. "We made it, though," he said. "We must have a guardian angel."

But Jack wasn't so sure. He felt the danger in his bones as the air pressure plummeted and his ears popped.

Suddenly, a gust of wind slammed into the lifeboat like a freight train. It grabbed the sail and shook it just like Jack shook rats to kill them.

"Hold on!" Chips called.

Jack heard a sharp crack. The mast snapped in two.

"Look out!" Julio cried.

The lifeboat's mast hurdled down, straight toward O'Brien.

Jack leaped, trying to knock the man out of harm's way.

O'Brien screamed as he fell to the bottom of the boat.

CHAPTER 18

Julio's hands shook as he helped Stewie tie the wooden splint around Chips's arm. The Irishman's face was white with pain.

"Ocean's calm as a kitten," Stewie said, shaking his head.

Julio nodded, looking up at the blue, cloudless sky. "I can't believe it's the very same ocean as yesterday," he said.

"But we're alive," Chips said through clenched teeth. "Help me into that life vest," he said. "If I get washed overboard, I'll not be able to swim."

Julio sighed. They may have escaped with their lives, but they were in a heck of a pickle: the mast was smashed to smithereens, so they couldn't sail the boat. Their first aid kit and most of their food was gone. The only food they didn't lose were the two things they didn't want: limes and pemmican.

And now there were just two of them to row. How would they ever make it to land?

Julio took his father's compass from his pocket. The fact that he hadn't lost it in the waves brought tears to his eyes. Out here, on this endless ocean in this tiny lifeboat, Julio felt closer to his father than he ever had.

"What's it say?" Chips O'Brien asked in a low voice.

Julio studied the compass. "Southwest. We're still heading southwest."

Julio thought it truly miraculous that the wind that had almost killed them had never sent them off their westward course.

"Good," O'Brien nodded.

"I better see if I can get Jamaica to drink some water," Stewie said.

Julio felt a cold dread at the mention of Jamaica's name. The events of the night before had taken every bit of strength he'd had.

Jack left Jamaica's side and walked weakly to Julio's. He glared at Chips and settled himself with a groan at Julio's feet.

O'Brien held up one hand. "I've got no quarrel with you, dog."

"You don't? I thought you hated Jack," Julio said. Even though he *did* save your life, Julio thought.

O'Brien shifted his weight and grimaced in pain. "I don't hate Jack in particular, just dogs in general."

"Why?"

O'Brien sighed. "When I was just a small lad in Ireland, I was put out to work in the factory. Every morning before the sun came up, I walked to work."

"I don't see what that has to do with hating dogs," Julio said stubbornly, rubbing Jack's ears.

Chips glanced at Jack and then away. "They found it amusing to set their dogs on a small Irish boy."

"That sounds bad," Julio said, "but Jack would never hurt a person. Another dog maybe, a rat definitely, but not a human."

Chips nodded. "He's a good one."

"Do all kids in Ireland have to work?" Julio didn't know a lot about Ireland except that it was supposed to be very green and have fairies.

"Kids who don't have parents to take care of them do," O'Brien said in a low voice.

Julio swallowed. "I don't have parents either. No family except for Jack and the crew on the *Susquehanna*."

Chips nodded. "I wondered why such a young lad was working as a cabin boy."

Julio shrugged. "It was a lot better than the orphanage. Everybody on the *Susquehanna* treated me and Jack really nice, like we were as much a part of the crew as anybody else." Unlike you, Julio thought.

"That was a brave thing you did, trying to save the food," Chips said. "You're a tough lad."

Julio looked away. The last thing he wanted was for O'Brien to see the tears in his eyes. "Yeah, but I failed." Just like all the times at the orphanage he'd tried and failed to belong, to have friends, to be the kid that got picked instead of picked *on.*

"Ah, but we have pemmican and limes," O'Brien said, with a smile. "What else does a man need?"

"Now there's an idea." Stewie said. He left Jamaica and came back to join Julio, Jack, and O'Brien. "Maybe if we squeeze lime juice on the pemmican, we'll be able to eat it."

"That sounds awful," Julio said, wrinkling his nose. "I'd never eat that."

"You'd be surprised what you'll eat when you're starving," Chips said.

Julio frowned. "Why do you keep saying that?"

If Chips O'Brien was a spy or a traitor, why would he know about starving?

Chips looked away. "Having three different ships torpedoed out from under me and spending two weeks in a lifeboat makes me an expert, lad."

"Holy mother," Stewie breathed. "Three ships?"

Chips nodded. "And now I suppose you'll be thinking I'm bad luck, along with being a gimpy Irishman?"

"No," Stewie said, admiration in his voice. "I'll

be thinking this man is a survivor. If he can make it, we can make it too."

"So that's how you knew that U-boat commander wouldn't shoot us?" Julio asked.

Chips nodded. "Most of them have no stomach for it. They're just following orders."

Relief washed over Julio. So Chips was not a spy or a traitor. "Did your leg get hurt one of those times your ship sank?"

Chips nodded. "Aye." And that was all he would say.

Stewie grabbed the tin of pemmican and bag of limes. He sliced open a lime and squeezed the juice onto the leathery paste of meat, oats, and dried fruit.

"Here goes." He closed his eyes and shoved the piece of food into his mouth. Everyone watched as he chewed and chewed and chewed. Finally, he swallowed.

"How is it?" Julio asked.

"I've had worse, but I can't for the life of me remember when."

Stewie handed the pemmican and bag of limes around. "Squeeze some lime into your water, too, for vitamin C," he directed. "We don't need to get sick from scurvy on top of everything else."

Julio shuddered at the word "scurvy." He'd read about it in the books on sailing in the library. The lack of vitamin C caused the early sailors to have bleeding gums, loose teeth, bulging eyes. Some men even died from it.

Julio squeezed lime juice into a cup of water and took it to Jamaica. His friend hadn't been eating; he hadn't been able to get him to drink that morning either. Julio knew that if Jamaica didn't drink more water, he'd die.

He held the cup of water to Jamaica's lips.

Jamaica smiled for the first time in days. "Home."

At first, Julio worried his friend was hallucinating from fever. But then he remembered the many stories the able seaman had told him about his home in Jamaica. Lime trees grew all over the island.

Julio tipped the cup and slowly poured water into Jamaica's mouth. "Straight from home," Julio said.

After he'd given Jamaica another cup of water,

Julio squeezed as much lime juice as he could into his own cup and on half of the pemmican. His eyes watered as he chewed the rubbery food. Stewie was right, the taste of pemmican and lime was terrible!

"Here, Jack." Julio held out the other half of the pemmican. "You need to eat too."

Jack sniffed the bar. He glared at Julio and went back to his bed.

"Look at that." Chips chuckled. "Even a dog won't eat it!"

But Julio didn't think it was a bit funny. Jack had never turned down something to eat, no matter what it was. He'd even eat vegetables!

Julio made his way over to Jack. He stroked his dog's head and ears. Jack hadn't been the same since he'd jumped into the ocean to rescue him. Now that he thought about it, Jack hadn't eaten since then. And he wasn't drinking much either.

Julio felt Jack shudder.

He stroked the dog's side. "What's wrong, Jack?" The sun beat down on them mercilessly, so he certainly couldn't be cold. Maybe he was too hot. He needed shade.

Julio pulled his hand away. Jack's hair covered his palm. Julio felt sick through and through.

He draped a wool blanket from one side of the lifeboat to the other, creating shade for his dog.

Jack sighed and licked his finger in thanks. Julio could see the misery in his dog's eyes.

"Oh, Jack," Julio whispered, "please don't leave me."

CHAPTER 19

Hours later, Jack woke from a fitful sleep. His boy was not beside him. He listened for the sound of Julio's voice. The boat was eerily quiet.

Jack sat up and searched the air for the scent of his boy. *There.*

Jack pulled himself out from under the shade of the blanket and into the sunlight.

He saw Stewie pulling on the oars, his shirtless chest and back burned by the sun. The man O'Brien groaned with pain every time he rowed with his one good arm.

Jack knew he should try to cheer the humans, but he was too tired. It took all the strength he had in his great heart to take care of his boy. Humans were a lot of work.

He followed the scent he knew as well as his own. He found Julio resting in a corner. His eyes were closed. One hand dangled over the edge of the boat. Jack stood next to his boy, watching. Something was not right, but the dog could not smell what was wrong.

Jack felt something move through the water. He peered over the side and saw the biggest fish he'd ever seen in his life. Dark, torpedo-shaped creatures swam beneath the boat. Two began circling it. One bumped the side of the boat near Julio's hand.

Too near for Jack's comfort.

The dog stood on his hind legs, paws braced on the rail, and barked a warning. *Stay away from my boy!*

Julio's eyes flew open. He jerked his hand back and peered over the edge.

"Sharks!" he screamed.

Danger! Jack barked over and over.

Stewie and O'Brien scrambled to their feet, almost capsizing the boat. Jack's front paws slipped on the slick wood, nearly dumping him into the water. He scrambled back, never taking his eyes from the evil things circling the boat.

Suddenly an especially large shark lunged from the water, mouth wide open. Jack froze. For just a second, he looked into the fathomless eye of the most fearful thing he had ever encountered. For just one heartbeat, Jack's steadfast bravery faltered.

"No!" Julio screamed as he brought his oar down hard on the shark's snout. The shark sank into the water and disappeared.

Jack's heart swelled with pride. His boy was so, so brave!

Another shark cruised so close to the boat, it scraped its side, pushing the lifeboat toward the other sharks.

Jack growled. Did these creatures not understand that this was *his* boat and these were *his* humans?

Stewie and O'Brien grabbed oars and slapped the shark away.

Jack saw a fin flash just beyond the bow. He'd had enough of these fish.

He jumped up onto the bow, barking and barking for the ugly creatures to leave his boat alone.

His front paws skittered and slipped on the wet wood. Before he could catch himself, he fell headfirst into the shark-infested sea.

Cold water closed over his head. He felt weightless yet heavy as he sank below the surface.

Something bumped him. His lungs cried out for air.

The instinct to survive drove his legs as he paddled quickly to the surface.

He saw the boat and the terrified face of his boy. He had to get back to him! Jack swam as hard as he could, his eyes fixed on Julio's.

He watched as Julio lay on his belly, reaching his hand out to Jack. He was close, so close!

A wave knocked him away from the boat.

"Somebody help me!" Jack heard the desperation in Julio's voice. "The sharks will get Jack!"

Jack felt movement far below him. He didn't dare look down. He just needed to get in the boat.

Jack saw Julio pull off his shoes. He knew what that meant.

No! he barked. Oh, his boy was brave, but he could be foolish too!

The man, Chips, agreed. He grabbed Julio around the waist. "No, lad."

Jack's heart filled with relief. One problem down. The next problem: his legs didn't seem to want to work anymore. Jack whimpered with fear.

Splash!

Jack yipped with surprise. It was the man, Chips, swimming toward him! He kicked his legs and paddled with his one arm. The man wasn't a much better swimmer than he was, but Jack could see the determination in Chips's eyes.

With one last burst of strength, Jack paddled for all he was worth to the man.

Jack felt a swirling in the water below.

"Look out!" he heard Julio cry.

Jack looked behind him. There, slicing through the water, was the dark triangular fin of a shark.

CHAPTER 20

SUNDAY, MAY 25, 1943
4:13 P.M. LOCAL TIME

To Julio's horror, the sharks wheeled and headed back toward the boat.

"Look out, they're coming back!" Julio cried.

"Help us!" Julio pleaded to Stewie, who stood watching, frozen.

Julio's words brought Stewie back to life. He grabbed an oar and beat the water. "We'll draw the buggers over this way," Stewie said.

Jamaica pushed off his blanket and, for the first time in days, sat up. He pulled himself to his knees. He clutched the wooden bucket and slammed it against the waves.

The sharks were almost upon Chips and Jack.

Chips grabbed Jack around his chest with his splinted arm. The dog clawed in blind panic, scratching the man's arms, despite the life vest.

"I'm trying to help you, you crazy dog."

Blood from the scratches on Chips's arm stained the water. Julio knew that in just a matter of seconds, the sharks would smell the blood.

Julio saw a long, dark form circling beneath Chips and Jack.

"Look out!" Julio yelled.

"Get us back in the boat!" O'Brien cried. "Now!"

"Grab the oar!" Stewie stretched out his arm as far as he could.

Chips grabbed onto the end of the oar with his good hand. "Pull!"

Just as Stewie pulled Chips and Jack alongside the boat, a shark lunged. With all his might, Julio slammed his oar against the head of the shark until the oar snapped in two. The shark spiraled downward, stunned.

Stewie and Jamaica reached down and pulled

Jack up and over the edge of the lifeboat.

A wave slapped the oar from Chips's hand.

"Get him!" Jamaica said.

Julio leaned off the side of the boat, almost slipping into the water himself. Stewie grabbed Julio's belt.

"Take my hand!" Julio said.

Chips kicked his way to Julio and clutched the boy's wrist with all his strength.

All three pulled the Irishman from the sea.

Everyone collapsed onto benches and blankets, spent.

Julio crouched next to Jack and Chips. He wiped back tears as he stroked Jack's side. "Oh, Jack, I almost lost you."

At the sound of his name, Jack raised his head from the man's chest and looked at his boy. He thumped his tail weakly and then licked the man—the man who had saved his life—on the face with thanks.

Chips opened his eyes. He half smiled at the dog. "I do believe Jack is Irish."

Julio frowned. "Why?" As far as he knew, boxers were not from Ireland.

Chips sat up and rubbed the top of the dog's broad head. "Because he's got the short temper, hard head, and brave heart of an Irishman."

Everyone laughed, even Jamaica.

"Let's get out of here," Stewie said, grabbing an oar. "I don't like the neighbors."

Chips reached for his oar and grimaced with pain.

"I'll take that," Julio said, sitting next to Chips.

Julio could barely speak around the knot in his throat. He could never, ever repay this man, but at least he could take his turn rowing.

Jack came over and curled up at their feet. He rested his head on O'Brien's foot.

"You lost your shoes," Julio pointed out.

Chips looked down at his feet and shrugged. "So I did."

Julio dipped the oar into the water, then pulled back. Dip, pull. Dip, pull.

"Sorry Jack ripped your shirt up," Julio said. Dip, pull. Dip, pull. "He didn't mean to. He was just scared."

Chips nodded. "He wasn't the only one."

Dip, pull. Dip, pull. Dip, pull.

Tears of gratitude and exhaustion slid down Julio's cheeks. "Thanks," he whispered.

Chips reached down and scratched Jack's ears. "He's a good lad."

And much to Julio's surprise, Chips slipped his good arm around Julio's shoulders and smiled.

"I need to wash that salt water out of my mouth," Chips said. "I'll get some water for Jack too."

Julio rowed, thinking how lucky they were that the sharks didn't get Jack or Chips. Maybe they did have a guardian angel after all.

"Blast!" Chips tossed blankets this way and bins and boxes that way.

"What's wrong?" Julio asked.

Chips looked shattered. "The water jug, it's gone!"

"Gone? How could it just disappear?" Stewie asked.

Chips sat down heavily on the bench. "It must have washed overboard during all the commotion."

Julio felt all hope drain from him. How long could they possibly survive without food or water?

CHAPTER 21

TUESDAY, MAY 27, 1943
11:23 P.M. LOCAL TIME

Julio looked up at the wide expanse of stars. The moon, just a sliver in the night sky, reflected down on the glassy ocean. The lifeboat rocked ever so gently in the water, like a cradle. Julio thought he might have the tiniest memory of his mother rocking him like this, but he wasn't sure.

The last two days had been brutal. Everyone had blisters, raw sores, and cracked lips from the searing sun and salt water. Julio and Stewie had tried to cover as much of the open boat as possible with the canvas sail—it was useless without a mast anyway—to shelter from the sun. Chip's arm was most likely broken, and Jamaica was barely conscious now. They had lost the first aid kit when the food was washed away. They still had the one the German commander had given them, but it was almost empty.

But still, they had to row. Despite the pain and the lack of food and water, they rowed west slowly. What else could they do? Julio wondered. Give up and die? Tears trickled down his face.

He took out his pocketknife and carved another notch into the wooden handle of his oar. He'd started doing this on the first night of their ordeal, to track the days. He ran his finger across the rough cuts, and counted. *One, two, three, four, five.* Five days they had been on this lifeboat. How many more could they expect to survive without food or water? How close or how far were they from land? They had no way of knowing.

Julio thought about the last time they were in port in Savannah. Had it really only been a few weeks ago?

As always, he and Jack had wandered the

familiar streets of the lovely town. Captain Bayne had given him his pay. "Don't spend it all in one place," he'd said like he always did.

Julio had bought a new pair of shoes for the colder weather. Then he and Jack went to the candy store. He'd wanted to buy a sack of his and Jamaica's favorite candies to share with the crew.

Inside, a young boy—about the age he'd been when his parents died, Julio reckoned—pointed to a large pinwheel sucker. "That one," he'd said. His mother had laughed, brushed the hair from the little boy's face, and said, "If that's what you want for your special birthday treat, then that's what you get, sugar."

Julio had left without his candy. He'd never been to a candy store with his mother or his father. He'd never really had a chance to be a kid, picking out special treats for his birthday.

And now he probably never would. Julio swallowed hard past this knot in his throat.

For the first time that day, Jack stirred at Julio's feet. His ears and nose twitched and searched. The dog was sick and exhausted from lack of food and water, but his eyes shone in the moonlight with curiosity.

Jack pulled himself to his feet and stared with fascination out into the distance. The hair stood on his back, then flattened. He whined a curious whine.

Julio silently prayed they were not about to be visited by sharks again.

"Do you hear it, son?" Chips asked from the back of the boat.

Julio stood, careful not to wake Stewie and Jamaica, and listened. And there, just barely, he heard an otherworldly song in the distance. It rose and fell, echoed and surrounded them.

"What is it?" Julio whispered.

"A humpback whale."

Julio had seen the giant whales once when the *Susquehanna* had carried supplies to Colombia and Venezuela months before. From the bridge, he and Captain Bayne had watched them leap almost clear of the water. It had seemed impossible for an animal so big. For several minutes, the pod of five whales had accompanied the ship as if providing an escort.

The haunting songs continued, only louder

now. The animals seemed to be moving closer.

Then, as if in a dream, the long, shining back of a whale appeared just a few yards from the lifeboat. A geyser of water shot into the air as the whale exhaled. A fishy-smelling spray drenched Julio and Jack.

Another whale appeared, and then another.

Julio knew he should be afraid: the whales could sink the lifeboat with just a flip of their tail. But Jack did not growl, nor did he seem worried. Only curious.

The whales swam slowly and, it seemed to Julio, carefully past the lifeboat. Only one whale lingered close to the boat. It was much smaller than the rest, a calf with a youngster's curiosity. It swam close to the side of the boat and rolled slightly on its side. One heavily lidded eye studied Julio's and Jack's faces as if memorizing them.

Jack whimpered like a small puppy and wagged his stump of a tail.

Julio stared back into the eye of the whale. He felt as if he could swim in that bottomless grayish blue and find the answers to all the questions he had ever had.

He reached out a hand, and just for the briefest moment, touched the wet skin. A calm of certainty filled Julio's spirit. Despite the odds, he knew somehow everything would be okay.

The whale blinked, rolled back to center, and disappeared beneath the sea.

CHAPTER 22

Jack lay next to his boy under the canvas sail. He stared through half-closed eyes at the shadows on the bottom of the boat. His tongue was swollen from thirst; he felt his heart racing as if he and Julio were running together on the shore. Boy oh boy, Jack thought, those were the best times. Him and his boy in port, exploring new places, new smells. Once his boy bought a kite. They raced up and down the beach, the kite flying high above, the gulls crying in annoyance. Jack wagged his tail at the memory. He could practically hear those birds now.

Screeeee! Scree! Screeeeee!

Jack's eyes flew open. Could those really have been birds? He hadn't seen or smelled birds in days.

A bird-shaped shadow skimmed across the bottom of the lifeboat. Jack pulled himself to his feet and staggered out into the early morning light.

Screeee! Screeeee!

Cormorants called from overhead.

Birds! Jack barked hoarsely. *Birds! Birds!*

"Somebody shut that dog up," Stewie growled.

Jack flared his nostrils open as wide as he could, searching the wind coming from the west. He knew from his time at sea that where there were birds, land was not far away.

His nose quivered. His nose searched for the smell of land. He leaned as far out over the front of the boat as he dared, trying to catch the scent.

Finally, he smelled it: the rich scent of earth and green growing things. It was far away, he knew, but it was there.

Jack scrambled back under the shelter. He

grabbed his boy's arm and pulled.

"Hey," Julio said, through cracked lips. "That hurts!" He yanked his arm away and rolled over onto his side.

Jack growled impatiently. Why didn't his boy listen to him?

Come see! Come smell! Jack barked, even though he knew humans could hardly smell a thing. He grabbed Julio's arm again and pulled him up. The boy seemed to weigh no more than a heavy stick.

Julio stumbled after Jack into the sunlight. Cormorants, frigate birds, and gulls filled the air.

"Birds," Julio whispered.

Birds! Jack yipped.

Chips O'Brien and Stewie crawled out from under the shelter.

"What in the blue blazes is all the ruckus about?" Stewie asked.

Look! Jack barked, jumping up and down. *Look!*

The men watched in wonder as seabirds circled, dipped, and swooped above.

"If there are birds, there must be land close by," Chips said, a grin splitting his sun-scorched face.

Jack saw a flicker of hope in the man's eyes.

"Where do you think it could be?" Julio asked. "How far away?"

"Some birds can fly hundreds of miles from land," Stewie said.

Jack smelled the disappointment in his boy.

"But even if we're not in sight of land," Julio said hopefully, "maybe we're close to fishing boats."

Jack sneezed with impatience. Why weren't they smelling land? It was plain as the tiny noses on their faces!

Then Jack felt it: the water near the lifeboat vibrated ever so slightly. He swiveled his tall, pointed ears one way and then the other, trying to catch the source of the thrum beneath his feet.

Finally, he saw it. A flash of light glinted off something in the distance. Something large and metal.

"Is that a ship?" Julio whispered in wonder.

Yes! Jack barked. *Yes! Yes! Yes!*

CHAPTER 23

"**A** ship!" Julio cried. "There's a ship!"

O'Brien squinted in the direction Julio pointed.

"Well, would you look at that," he said. "It is a ship."

They studied the shape in the distance. The sun shone off the sides of the vessel and illuminated a tall white sail.

"How do we know it's not an enemy ship?" Stewie said.

"Who cares," Julio said. "Even prisoners are

given water and a piece of bread." He jumped up and down, waving his arms and screaming, "Here! Over here!"

Jack joined in, barking and jumping too.

The lifeboat rocked wildly. Water poured over the side.

O'Brien grabbed Julio. "Stop your jumping, lad, before you get us all killed!"

"Why the heck did Captain Bayne have to forget the flare guns?" Stewie moaned. "They'll never see us out here."

Julio snapped his finger. "But we do have a signal mirror!" He scrambled under the bench of the boat.

"Here," he said, holding it up in triumph. "We'll signal them with this."

Stewie grabbed the mirror from Julio and held it up to the sun, moving it back and forth.

"That's not how you do it," Julio said.

"And you know how?" Stewie snapped.

"Yeah," Julio said. "I read about it in a library book."

Julio pointed the mirror toward his oar. Slowly, he brought the mirror up to his eye and

tilted it toward the sun.

"There," he said, letting out a breath. "I've got a bead of light."

Keeping the bead of light on the surface of the mirror, Julio pointed it toward the boat in the distance. Quickly, he flashed the mirror three times.

"That's the international signal for distress," Julio explained.

Everyone, even Jack, held their breath, waiting for some sign the boat had seen their signal.

"Try it again, lad," O'Brien said.

Flash, flash, flash.

The boat turned slowly east.

"No!" Stewie cried. "They're going the wrong way!"

O'Brien squeezed Julio's shoulder. "Again."

Julio closed his eyes. He thought about all they'd been through and how hard they'd tried.

Jack licked his fingertips. Julio looked into the eyes of his best friend and saw the trust and the confidence and, most of all, the love.

Julio flashed the mirror again three times, waited ten seconds and flashed the signal again.

Nothing.

CHAPTER 24

Then suddenly, the front of the ship swung around. Its nose pointed toward the lifeboat.

"I think they see us!" Stewie cheered.

No one needed to tell Julio to flash the mirror again. He flashed three times, waited ten seconds, and then sent the distress signal again. Over and over and over.

The ship slowly grew larger.

"They see us!" Julio whooped. "They see us! They see us!"

Julio scrambled over to Jamaica. Gently, he

shook his friend's arm. "Hey, hey, Jamaica," he said.

Slowly, the man opened his eyes. He searched Julio's face.

"There's a boat coming," Julio said. "We're going to be rescued!"

Jamaica took Julio's hand and squeezed it with surprising strength.

The boat closed in, close enough that they could see the flag flying at the top of the mast: a yellow diamond on a green background with a blue globe in the middle.

"It's Brazilian!" Stewie shouted. "It's a Brazilian flag!"

"Judging from the nets, it looks like a fishing boat," O'Brien said.

"Don't care what kind of boat it is, long as they got water," Stewie said.

Stewie hugged Julio so hard, Julio thought he'd surely crack his ribs. "You sure saved our hide, Julio."

Julio's heart swelled with pride.

"Jack was the one that spotted the boat first

though," he said. "We would have missed it without him."

Jack wagged his tail at the sound of his name.

The boat pulled up a few feet from the lifeboat. Four men and a young boy studied the ragtag crew of the *Susquehanna*. The tallest of the men glared at the oars in their hands.

"Drop your oars," O'Brien ordered in a low voice. The oars clattered to the bottom of the lifeboat.

"Any of you speak English?" O'Brien called.

The fishermen looked at each other and shook their heads.

"What language do they speak in Brazil?" Stewie asked.

"I think it's Portuguese," Julio said, recalling the *Susquehanna*'s supply run to South America.

"You speak Portuguese?" O'Brien asked Stewie.

Stewie shrugged.

"I speak a little," Julio said. He liked learning new languages when they spent a day or two in a new country.

Julio reached back in his memory. Captain Bayne had told Julio that Brazil was a close ally of America. He needed to let them know they were friends.

"*Somos Americanos.*"

The fishermen's faces opened just a bit.

"Tell them we need help. We're starving and thirsty," Stewie said.

Julio didn't know all those words. He said, "*Nos,* um, *nos* need *ajuda.*" He rubbed his stomach and held an imaginary cup to his lips. "Hungry," he said. "Thirsty."

The young boy waved at Julio. "Food? Water?"

"Yes!" Julio said. "Yes! Food! Water! *Ajuda!*"

"Ship lost?" the boy asked.

Julio nodded. "Yes, lost." He held up his hands. "Six days. Lost six days."

The boy talked excitedly to the fishermen.

The next thing they knew, the men threw lines into the lifeboat and pulled their boat alongside.

Arms and hands reached down to lift them up.

"Jamaica first," Julio said.

Carefully, Stewie lifted Jamaica in his arms as if he were a child. With Chips's help, they handed their friend to safety.

"Grab whatever you need from the boat and let's get out of here," O'Brien said.

Julio looked back at the boat that had been their home for the last six days. He checked his pocket for his knife and compass. He called Jack to his side.

"I've got everything I need," he said.

CHAPTER 25

"It's your turn, Julio."

Julio blinked and looked down at the cards in his lightly bandaged hands. The bandages were fresh and white. White as the nurses' uniforms and the bedsheets in the Salvador City Hospital.

Five days had passed since the fishing boat had found them and brought them to the hospital in the city of Salvador. Wounds were cleaned and stitched, bodies bathed and outfitted in clean hospital pajamas, and spirits restored. Food had

never tasted so good, water so divine. And best of all, Jamaica was going to be okay. Wasn't that enough?

Still, Julio wondered, why did he feel so sad?

Chips tapped Julio's knee with his cards.

"What's going on in that head of yours, son?"

Julio shrugged and looked away. How could he explain all the doubt and joy and confusion inside him? After all he'd been through, after what he and Jack had survived, why was he terrified?

Chips leaned in. "Julio?"

Julio took a deep breath. "I just don't know . . ." He trailed off.

"Know what?"

"I just don't know what happens now," he said. "For me and Jack." What if he got sent to another orphanage? What would happen to Jack?

Chips smiled and patted Julio's shoulder. "Neither do I, lad, but I think whatever it is, we should figure it out together."

Julio looked up, his eyes wide with surprise. "You mean 'we' as in, you and me?"

Chips nodded. "We've been through a lot together," he said. "And I haven't always done right by you." Chips looked down at his cards. "I don't have any family, but I think it would be a fine thing." He looked at Julio, blue eyes into brown. "I'd be proud to count you as family, Julio, that is, if it's okay with you."

Chips smiled at the boxer sleeping at the foot of Julio's bed. "And of course, Jack too."

Julio rubbed his thumb over his father's compass. It couldn't tell him which way to go now, only his heart could. And his heart felt full with hope.

Julio tapped his chin, pretending to give the matter a great deal of thought. "I don't know," he said. "I don't think I want to go to sea anytime soon." He shook his finger at the Irishman. "And I happen to know you snore."

Chips laughed a big, full-belly laugh. "I have no intention of setting foot on a boat again, except to get back to America! And you think *I* snore? That dog of yours saws logs like a lumberjack!"

The two laughed and looked at the brown-and-white dog, belly up and legs sprawled.

"What do you think, Jack?" Julio said, rubbing the dog's belly. "Should we throw in our lot with a gimpy Irishman?"

CHAPTER 26

MONDAY, JUNE 2, 1943
6:40 P.M. LOCAL TIME

Jack smelled the happiness between Julio and Chips. He felt a hope in his boy that had been missing for a long time. He hadn't always liked the man called Chips, hadn't trusted him any more than he'd trusted that cat. But Jack remembered the man's strong arms pulling him back into the boat, saving his life twice. And now, he made Julio happy. From anger and meanness to kindness and love.

Humans sure are funny animals, Jack thought.

"What do you think, Jack?" Julio said, rubbing Jack's belly. "Should we throw in our lot with a gimpy Irishman?"

Jack wagged his stump of a tail. He yipped with joy. *Yes!*

SHIPWRECK ON THE HIGH SEAS Q&A

Did dogs like Jack really live aboard ships during World War II?

Yes, they certainly did! As a matter of fact, all kinds of animals—dogs, cats, pigs, goats, parrots, and even a bear—lived and worked with the crew on military ships throughout the world. They served many functions aboard ship: rat killer, early warning system, defender, message deliverer, and morale booster. Like Jack, most of the animal mascots were strays adopted by the crew. Often, these animals were made honorary crew members, complete with their own uniforms and tailor-made life jackets. The role of the mascot was part symbol of the crew's unity, part comic relief, part good luck charm, and one hundred percent friend.

The character of Jack was inspired by two real-life seafaring dogs during World War II, Sinbad and Judy.

MEET A REAL HERO DOG

JUDY

NATIONALITY: BRITISH

BREED: POINTER

JOB: MASCOT ABOARD HMS *GRASSHOPPER* AND HMS *GNAT*

STRENGTHS: LOYALTY, BRAVERY, KEEN HEARING

STATIONED: YANGTZE AND SINGAPORE

HEROIC MOMENT: SAVED SEVERAL DROWNING PASSENGERS WHEN THE SS *VAN WARWYCK* WAS TORPEDOED. THE ONLY DOG REGISTERED AS AN OFFICIAL PRISONER OF WAR DURING WORLD WAR II.

HONORS: PDSA DICKIN MEDAL, BRITAIN'S HIGHEST HONOR.

TOP TEN SEAFARING ANIMAL FACTS

1. Nearly 15,000 years ago, the Phoenicians took cats aboard their ships to keep down the rat population. Later, the Vikings did the same. A few thousand years later, the Romans took chickens aboard their military ships to predict the outcome of battles!

2. A dog's sense of smell is almost 100 million times more sensitive than a human's, making them perfect for sniffing out rats!

3. A dog's sense of hearing is beyond superhuman! They can hear four times the distance that a human can, and a much wider range of frequencies. During wartime, they acted as "early warning systems" since they were able to hear the approach of enemy aircraft well before the human crew members.

4. Dogs such as the British Royal Navy's mascot, Judy, were often used for hunting when in port. Judy also defended her human crew members when river pirates boarded their patrol boat.

5. Judy was the only dog during World War II to be officially declared a prisoner of war by the Japanese.

6. Sinbad served through combat with the Germans and Japanese on the US Coast Guard cutter *Campbell*.

7. Tirpitz the pig started out as a mascot aboard a German ship. When that ship was sunk by a British ship during the Battle of the Falkland Islands, he swam to the British ship and was adopted by the crew!

8. Oskar the cat survived the sinking of three different ships, both German and British, earning him the nickname "Unsinkable Sam." Now that's a cat with nine lives!

9. For centuries, goats have provided fresh milk and cheese on military ships. Goats were perfect for long voyages at sea because they were small, ate almost anything, and could swim!

10. Perhaps the most important job of seafaring mascots was that of nonjudgmental friend on the long, grueling, dangerous voyages during wartime.

TIMELINE OF

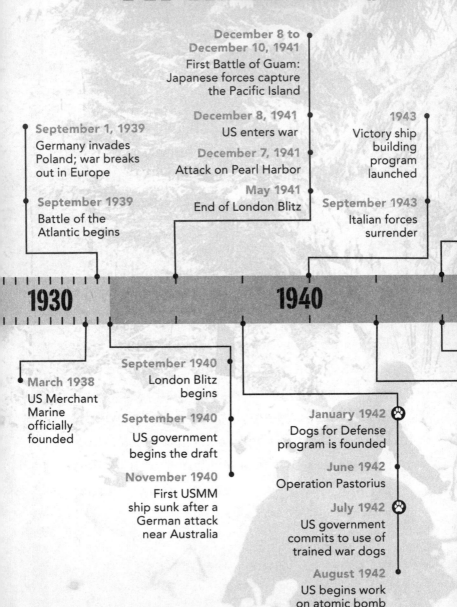

December 8 to December 10, 1941
First Battle of Guam: Japanese forces capture the Pacific Island

September 1, 1939
Germany invades Poland; war breaks out in Europe

September 1939
Battle of the Atlantic begins

December 8, 1941
US enters war

December 7, 1941
Attack on Pearl Harbor

May 1941
End of London Blitz

1943
Victory ship building program launched

September 1943
Italian forces surrender

1930

1940

March 1938
US Merchant Marine officially founded

September 1940
London Blitz begins

September 1940
US government begins the draft

November 1940
First USMM ship sunk after a German attack near Australia

January 1942
Dogs for Defense program is founded

June 1942
Operation Pastorius

July 1942
US government commits to use of trained war dogs

August 1942
US begins work on atomic bomb

WORLD WAR II

May 8, 1945
V-E Day (Victory in Europe)

May 7, 1945
German forces surrender

May 1945
Battle of the Atlantic ends

August 1950
USMM ships are still being damaged by leftover German mines

January 1988
USMM servicemembers who served in World War II are officially recognized as veterans

1950 1960 1970 1980

June 6, 1944
D-Day at Normandy in France

July 21, 1944 to August 8, 1944
Second Battle of Guam: US takes control from Japan

August 25, 1944
Paris is freed from German control

August 6, 1945
Atomic bomb dropped on Hiroshima

August 9, 1945
Atomic bomb dropped on Nagasaki

August 14, 1945
Japanese forces surrender

September 2, 1945
V-J Day (Victory in Japan), Japanese sign surrender agreement

Q&A ABOUT THE MERCHANT MARINE

Q. What is the US Merchant Marine?
A. The US Merchant Marine was officially founded on March 15, 1938. During wartime, the merchant marine provides the crucial service of moving supplies—from food to tanks—to our troops and allied troops. During World War II, Liberty ships and Victory ships from ports in the United States delivered to troops all over the world. Their motto was "We deliver the goods."

Q. How many merchant marines were there during World War II?
A. In 1940, the merchant marine numbered about 55,000 men. After the United States entered the war in 1942, President Franklin D. Roosevelt realized that, in order to win the war, we needed many ships to carry much-needed supplies. A massive recruitment campaign almost tripled that number to 215,000!

Q. Who could be a merchant marine?

A. Practically anybody! Unlike other branches of the armed forces, the merchant marine did not have the same age and physical requirements. During World War II, the US Maritime Service officially accepted boys as young as sixteen and men as old as seventy-eight! Men who could not pass the physical requirements to serve in other branches of the military were welcomed into the merchant marine. They took volunteers with one eye, one leg, or even heart problems. Retired seamen were especially encouraged to come out of retirement to join the merchant marine since they'd require very little training.

The crew of a Liberty or Victory ship was probably the most racially diverse and integrated branch in the whole US military. Even a few women served as merchant marines!

Q. What was daily life on a merchant marine ship like?

A. Every person on the ship had their job. The ship's carpenter, always nicknamed Chips, built temporary and permanent things for the ship as well as making sure parts of the rigging were in good operating order. The men in the engine room stoked the fires in the boilers, oiled the machinery, and kept it clean. The cooks and bakers in the ship's kitchen, the galley, had the very important job of keeping everyone fed. During downtime, the crew read, played cards and dice, and wrote letters home. And, of course, everyone was assigned a four-hour watch shift every day. Emergency drills were also held daily. At sea, the crew's lives depended on the rapidity of an individual's response in an emergency—which could be anything from enemy threats to life-threatening storms.

Q. Was being a merchant marine dangerous?
A. Very dangerous! From the time they left a given port, they could be attacked by battleships, submarines, bombers, kamikaze planes, and sea mines. Because Liberty ships traveled slower than most ships, they were easy hits for the enemy. And because they were carrying supplies, the lifeline of any fighting army, they were important targets.

Q. Did German U-boats really help those stranded in lifeboats, or did you make that up?

A. They often did offer some help to survivors after torpedoing their ship. Although Hitler wanted the U-boats to kill as many merchant marines as possible, even gunning them down in lifeboats if necessary, the vast majority of U-boat commanders had no stomach for killing survivors of sinking ships. Very often they would give them food, water, chocolate, and cigarettes. They would also check the accuracy of the compass the survivors had and give them directions to the nearest land. The U-boat ace, Otto Kretschmer, posted a standing order on his U-boat that read in part, "Survivors are to be assisted if there is time. The crew of U-99 would expect to be rescued by the enemy, and that is precisely what the enemy have the right to expect from us."

Q. You talk about Liberty ships and Victory ships. What's the difference?

A. Liberty ships were the first supply ships built at the beginning of the war. Although they were big and could carry a lot of supplies (even tanks and airplanes!), they were slow. This is because they were powered by a steam engine. They averaged about 11 knots per hour. This made Liberty ships easy targets for the enemy. In 1943, the US Maritime Commission had a new, faster ship designed with a steam turbine engine. This ship could cruise at 15–17 knots—much faster than the Liberty ships! The Victory ships were also slightly larger and more streamlined than the "ugly duckling" Liberty ships.

TOP TEN MERCHANT MARINE STATS

1. Approximately 250,000 men served in the US Merchant Marine during World War II.

2. Between 1942 and 1945, 2,710 Liberty ships were built. This is easily the largest number of ships ever built from a single design. Starting in 1943, 531 Victory ships were built.

3. The Liberty ship SS *Robert E. Peary* was built in 4 days, 15 hours, and 29 minutes!

4. Liberty ships and their crew traveled over 6,000 miles of ocean to battlefronts in the Far East.

5. US Merchant Marine captains had orders to destroy their records and let their ships sink if they were about to be captured by an enemy vessel.

6. A Liberty ship could carry 10,200 tons of supplies!

7. 9,300 mariners lost their lives at sea during World War II. The US Merchant Marine had the highest casualty rate of all the branches in the military.

8. 663 mariners (men and women) were taken as prisoners of war.

9. 144 mariners were awarded the Distinguished Service Medal for service beyond the call of duty.

10. 362 mariners were awarded the Meritorious Service Medal for outstanding conduct or service.

Who Were the Flying Tigers?

In 1937, China and Japan were at war. The Japanese wanted to expand their empire by taking over parts of northern China. The takeovers were brutal; thousands of Chinese were killed.

When the war first began in 1931, the United States mostly stayed on the sidelines. The United States did have trade with China and missionaries there, but President Franklin Roosevelt was reluctant to get involved. However, in December 1937, Japanese aircraft attacked and sank the American gunboat, the USS *Panay*, in the Yangtze River in China. It was time for the United States to intervene.

Retired US Army Air Corps officer Claire L. Chennault had worked in China for several months before the attack on the USS *Panay* as military aviation advisor and director of the Chinese Air Force flight school. As part of this effort to help defend China against the invading Japan, Chennault formed the First American Volunteer Group of the Chinese Air Force. They would later be nicknamed the Flying Tigers. The nose of the fighter planes was painted with the image of the open jaws of a shark with fierce eyes.

The group was composed of pilots from the United States Army Air Corp as well as other branches of the US military. Their aircraft were marked with the Chinese colors but flew under American control under the command of Claire L. Chennault.

The group trained in Burma to defend China against Japanese forces. However, it wasn't until the United States entered the war, after the Japanese attack on Pearl Harbor, that the Flying Tigers first saw combat. Although the Flying Tigers were only in combat for a little over a year, they were very successful. Not only did they help beat back the Japanese assault on China, they gave hope to America and its allies that the Japanese could be defeated.

Read them all!

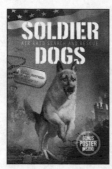

Love dogs?
You may also like...

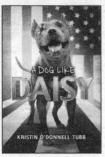